The Last Keeper

by

L. D. Nash

The Last Keeper

Cover Art by *Jennifer Greeff*

The Wild Rose Press, Inc.
PO Box 708
Adams Basin, NY 14410-0708
Visit us at www.thewildrosepress.com

Publishing History
First Edition, 2023
Trade Paperback ISBN 978-1-5092-4904-6
Digital ISBN 978-1-5092-4905-3

Published in the United States of America

She stomped up the stairs and slammed her bedroom door, keenly aware that she was acting like a spoiled teenager. Well, wasn't that what she was? No, she was a spoiled demoness. That's what she was. How could she be a demon? She didn't feel like a demon. She didn't want to eat small children or drown old ladies. She felt like herself, in all aspects but one. She examined her feelings for Penn. She'd never felt like this before, so she had nothing to compare it to. What if it was the demon in her wanting to seduce the angel in him?

She'd been in Sunday school enough to remember the teachings, and one of the big ones—demons tempted angels to fall. So, were her feelings true, or were they a manifestation of something deeper, darker, and slightly evil? There was no way to know unless she pursued them. The mere thought of having a relationship with Penn set her blood on fire. Lava coursed through her veins.

Could she come to love him? Should she love him? Those were questions she desperately wanted answers to. She wanted him for sure. Who wouldn't with a body like his?

Chapter 1

December 21, 2016

Warmth flooded Penn's skin. Every hair covering his body reacted by standing in shocky strands. A full-body shiver flicked the odd sensation from his skin like droplets of water from a duck's back, and he glanced at the girl standing to his left. This awareness wasn't like anything he'd ever felt during his time.

If asked to use words to describe the impression, he'd say it was as if his skin had burst to life and now hummed with unspent energy, kind of like a guitar string vibrated after being plucked.

Not even in his true angelic form had he ever felt so sensitized.

The word "love" popped into his mind, but he dismissed it as just a crazy thought. He couldn't know love because he'd sworn off love centuries ago when all his brethren had to watch their loved ones so cruelly murdered. He'd vowed that he'd never go through anything close to what they'd suffered that day. Love wasn't in their DNA. They were created to be alone. So, alone he'd remained, and alone he'd remain until the end.

He blamed the odd phenomenon on the old man disguise he'd donned instead of some crazy notion. Elderly human men were forever complaining about something or another. The wrinkled-up old dude wasn't his first choice as a disguise. He'd had to make a split-second decision to get a more personal look at the girl. Donning the appearance of a gravedigger had allowed him to get within arm's reach, but he couldn't just snatch her up and run.

Hell, he hoped she was the right one. Centuries of research pointed directly at her. Only by pure luck had he discovered her whereabouts a few days ago, or they'd all be up shit creek—without boat or paddle.

He'd just chalk it up to bad luck that he'd been sent to collect her while she was attending her parents' funeral.

Livy—or Olivia as was her true name—hadn't thought clearly enough to pay attention to a decrepit old machine operator.

Penn snuck covert glances at her face while he operated the machine, dumping dirt on the freshly dug graves. Tears and sadness shrouded her face in a black veil of mourning. She wore her chestnut-brown hair in a short, pixie style. The spiky ends softened the sharp angles of her cheekbones. Delicate brow bones arched perfectly across large eyes. Her lineage was shown in her features.

Only someone trained to search for these differences would even notice them. Other humans would just consider her uniquely beautiful. If he'd had to describe her in one simple word, "exotic" nailed it.

Her lime-green eyes glistened with unshed tears, and yet he still saw an otherworldly luminescence cocooning them. Thick, ebony eyelashes fanned the almond-sloped orbs like a preening peacock's tail feathers, and a pert little nose rested above full, plump lips.

His gaze lingered on those lips long enough to notice she'd either licked or chewed at the pale-pink lipstick until only the outer rim still held some color.

He caught the slight swivel of her head but was too engrossed by her beauty to realize he'd been busted. She'd noticed that he'd stopped shoveling and lifted those green eyes to glare up at him. She scowled when she caught him staring at her, her lips thinning in a hard, angry line.

Great, now she probably thought he was some dirty old pervert.

Penn powered down the tractor and offered a slight smile in hopes of buffering some of her emotions.

Suggest she explores the secluded corner of the cemetery. We need to know if she's the one. Sem's voice brushed through Penn's mind. *And stop imagining her warming your bed before I barf.*

Okay, all right. Jeez, you're such a buzz-kill, Penn confessed. He felt like he'd just been busted for fondling himself in public. *I can't help that I find her so interesting.*

So long as you remember that, although interesting, she's more than likely our only hope for the war ahead, Sem shot back.

****

Watching a machine dump soil on your mom and dad's coffins wasn't a great way to start the day. Livy had lost count of the hands she'd shaken and the half-hearted hugs she'd suffered thus far. Countless faces had passed before her, murmuring condolences and sympathies for her losses. Some told her that grief got easier with time, while others said to take her time and

3

mourn.

Honestly, everything was pretty much a blur, one action blending into another until she wasn't sure what she was doing.

Right up until a strange, old man began throwing dirt on her parents' coffins. He operated the tractor-like machine, a huge bucket on the front, with fluid expertise. The heavy thud of dirt hitting the coffins finally snapped her back to reality.

It felt like a dream, a crazy, depressing dream. The air surrounding her was soupy thick, her lungs laboring to breathe, and every moment passed in agonizing, slow motion. Studying the shiny walnut boxes covered with dirt forced her to admit that it was all real, and in surrendering to that knowledge, her tears gushed even stronger.

Her chest constricted; it filled with so much pain, she felt like she wanted to explode. But she stood firm and did her best to hold it all together.

She knew it was what her mom and dad would've wanted.

"Miss?"

From the corner of her eye, she spotted someone approaching her. Lifting her eyes, she faced them. The elderly man had called to her and now stood before her, his voice soft, respectful, and slightly hesitant.

Dabbing at her eyes with a tissue, she couldn't find her voice to respond, so she settled for a simple nod of her head.

"Miss?" he repeated, his bushy eyebrows furrowing slightly.

"Livy," she rasped. "My name is Livy." There, she'd found a few words. Maybe they were enough to build a conversation around. Then again, maybe he didn't want to talk, and that was fine with her.

"This isn't something a loved one should watch, miss," he announced, completely ignoring the fact she'd just told him her name. "Perhaps you'd like to take a walk while I finish?"

She frowned, his rudeness bothering her more than it should. Usually, when someone introduced themselves, the other person returned the gesture.

"The family doesn't usually watch this," he continued, gesturing between the machine and twin holes. A harsh laugh escaped her lips before she thought better, and the gesture solicited a frown from the man. He had no way of knowing she had nowhere else to go, nowhere to be, and no matter how far away she went, this memory would haunt her forever. Her entire life now rested six feet under.

Where else was she supposed to be? Her parents were her only family. Suddenly, it hit her like a bolt of lightning. She'd been orphaned at twenty years old.

"Miss?" the man pressed.

"I don't know where else to go," she whispered. The words automatically poured from her lips. She hadn't meant to say such a thing, but for some inexplicable reason, the man's mere presence elicited her secret.

She slowly lifted her eyes to his and barely caught the softening of his mouth. His forehead crinkled when he frowned again, and suddenly she felt utterly stupid. Legally, she was a grown woman. However, right now she acted like a lost little girl.

She shook her head, shifting herself away from him, the thought of fleeing propelling her feet to move.

He stopped her by placing his hand on her forearm. A strange warmth flooded her body, his touch turning her to molten lava. She'd never experienced such a reaction to anyone's touch. It was like her body recognized his. She wanted to feel revolted, but her body wouldn't let her.

"You could take a walk," he offered in a gentle tone and gestured to his right, where an old rusty gate, completely covered with English ivy, hung haphazardly from one broken hinge.

Snapping out of her reaction, she wanted to refuse, but then something nudged her forward. She felt like an invisible rope had settled around her waist, and it pulled her toward the gate and whatever lay beyond. She tugged her arm from his grasp and walked toward the portal, ducking her head to avoid some low-hanging vegetation.

"There's some beautiful statuary in that section," he called after her. "Not many folks visit them anymore." His voice trailed off, but she didn't turn to acknowledge him, and she forgot about the skin-to-skin reaction. Instead, her attention was completely stolen by the scene just beyond the gated entrance.

The moment her foot touched down on the other side of the gate, the atmosphere changed. The air thinned, the light faded, and shadows danced through the moss-covered live oaks. Old gravestones stood like defeated soldiers across the uneven ground. She glanced at the headstone to her left and read the date of death as 1759.

A sense of déjà-vu washed over her, and a wave of dizziness had her head spinning. A few seconds passed while she stood in the suspended study and imagined her feet sinking into the soft soil underneath her. It was as if she'd sprouted roots and couldn't turn and leave if she wanted to.

Belonging filled her soul, and a blanket of peace draped across her shoulders, replacing the heaviness of sorrow she'd carried since her parents' deaths three days ago. It was as if she was meant to be here, at this moment.

Looking around, she studied some of the other stones, and grief reemerged, the severity overwhelming her. She felt like she'd entered a land the living had thrown away and forgotten. None of the graves showed signs of being tended, and she made a mental note to speak with the caretaker before she left. Scraggy vegetation climbed up some of the gravestones, while others were black with years of mold. Moss hung from the oaks' branches, their tails wagging in the breeze. The grass was overgrown to the point it looked like no one had stepped foot in here for years.

The dead deserved just as much respect as the living.

The thought rushed through her mind, and a strong sense of conviction followed. She vowed to never abandon her mom and dad's graves like this. Even if she had to come every day, they would never end up overgrown with moss and weeds; they'd never succumb to the ravages of time.

A slight breeze swept through the moss-covered oaks, blowing a crisp brown leaf into her face. She reached up to remove it when a bright streak of light reflected off something in the distance to her left. She squinted through the erratic sun rays shining toward her and noticed that this section of the cemetery was much larger than she'd originally thought. The narrow gate opening and trail were deceiving as to what truly lay beyond.

Without thought or plan, she started in the direction she'd seen the light. She tip-toed, careful not to step on any graves, and followed the gentle slope of terrain as it carried her down into a small valley of sorts. Broken stone markers littered the ground when the appearance of plots just abruptly stopped. She felt like she'd crossed some invisible barrier that allowed no more graves.

Standing in a shallow crater—surrounded by a circle of at least six feet of dead grass—stood a solitary, stone angel. Not counting the three-foot-high pedestal, the statue stood at least four feet taller than Livy's five-foot-six inches. The rising sun cast a halo of bright light behind the angel, sending rays of red, orange, and yellow cascading out around her in a colorful arc. Like staring directly into the face of the sun, the sting of tears almost blinded Livy when they filled her eyes.

Blinking her misty eyes, she stepped closer, the dried grass crunching underneath her feet. She tilted her head back and gazed up into the angel's downturned face. A light sprinkling of green moss rested across the top of the statue's head and shoulders, and the tip of one of her wings was missing a healthy chunk. The other wing housed a rather large crack across the fan of feathers so detailed that they could be real.

Her face was eternally frozen in a serene mask of sorrow, her perfectly arched brows furrowed and her lips slightly parted.

The statue's folded arms, each hand holding the forearm of the other, gave the illusion that she hugged herself. Her long hair cascaded in loose curls to her waist, and she wore a long flowing robe, its numerous folds trapping leaves and other natural debris. The hemline of her robe covered her feet and the top of the blank pedestal.

Livy studied the space below the statue's feet and wondered if there should be a name or epitaph. She frowned at seeing it was simply bare; the artist didn't wish to claim his or her work.

Livy wished she knew more about the lonesome figure, shrouded in sadness and disrepair. Was the statue a likeness of someone interred here? Who was the talented artist who created such a treasure? Was she a mere decoration, or did she mark a grave? If she was a grave marker, then why was the ground around her bare of other plots? Why was the rest of the cemetery covered in a carpet of thick, green grass, and yet a circle of brown surrounded her?

The wind shifted, and the bright light winked again. This time Livy's eyes zeroed in on the source, and she realized it was a spot on the angel's right hand. Stepping even closer, bracing her hand on the pedestal for balance, Livy inspected the statue's hand, disappointed when she saw nothing that would cause the bright reflection.

The angel wore nothing but a plain band on her ring finger, but it was the same color stone as the rest of the statue, nothing bright or shiny that would explain the refraction of light. Livy frowned in confusion and reached out to tentatively touch the ring. The moment the pad of her finger stroked the cool, granite band, the world around her erupted in a fiery burst of chaos.

A gale-force wind rushed over her, slicking her

hair against her head. Her dress flattened to her body, revealing every curve. The powerful current of air was strong enough to knock her to the ground. Reaching up, Livy gripped the statue with both hands to keep herself from being thrown around like a weightless rag doll.

Dark red streaks bled into the formerly cloudless sky. Depthless tendrils spider-veined across the blue like fresh ichor. Smoke rushed across the terrain, blanketing the holy ground in a shroud of malevolence, and tiny fog particles filled the air around her. Balls of fire soared overhead, leaving trails of embers in their wake. Deafening explosions resounded when they collided with the earth, the hot lava destroying everything the flames touched. The ground shook every time a new fireball touched down. Panic clogged her throat and her breath shot out in short bursts.

Looking around, her eyes widened with shock. *What was happening?* It was like the apocalypse had hit like a tsunami. Heat rose from everywhere around her, scalding smoke emerging from earth's every pore, and yet the stone beneath her hands was ice cold. A deafening crack whipped through the air, and she turned in the direction of the sound.

Her eyes widened when the porous exterior of the angel before her spider-webbed into a series of deep cracks and crevices. Suddenly the entire statue shimmered like a frozen DVD and then exploded, sending time-weathered flecks of rock raining down atop her.

An onslaught of voices filled her head, thousands of pleas and cries, each one wailing for help. She winced as they ravished her mind like nails on a chalkboard. After minutes of agonizing torture, one emerged, standing out among the rest: a woman who sounded both terrified and relieved at the same time. She screamed for Livy to help her, to free her from her prison. Livy shook her head, and tears filled her eyes. Every other voice became nothing but background noise, and she frowned when she realized she was unable to distinguish any of the others.

Only hers.

A burning desire to help this woman overrode the shock and panic, the heated emotion boiling Livy's blood. Then a vision erupted inside her head, and she saw a cage, roughly the size of an SUV, completely wrapped in glowing steel chains.

A large padlock clamped the door closed.

That enormous cage held a lone white dove and she couldn't help but think the pen was so big—too big—for such a small animal. The tiny bird rested on her side in what looked like a small pool of blood. One wing jutted out in an awkward position. Somehow, Livy knew the fragile appendage was broken. She couldn't explain how she knew. The certainty was just there.

She summoned every ounce of determination within her and commanded the door to open. She *saw* it open. The padlock crumbled to dust, the chains fell to the ground, and the door swung open. The little bird struggled to its feet and weakly made its way free of the cruel cage. Once its body was free of the steel, it erupted into blinding white light, and its now pristine body appeared directly before Livy, both wings—completely healed—beating in unison.

Their eyes met and Livy felt the bird's gratitude. With every flap of the little creature's wings, the smoke surrounding them cleared farther and farther away until all the smoke was gone.

Thank you, Livy heard a woman's voice in her mind again. *I am indebted to you. There are many more of us. Please free my brothers and sisters as you have freed me.*

Livy opened her mouth, intending to tell the bird that she didn't understand, when the vision faded, and she once again stood before an undamaged statue. Reaching out, she placed her hand on the smooth surface, her brows furrowing in confusion.

Suddenly the effigy exploded, again, in a deafening roar. The blast sent her sprawling to the ground a few yards away. Shards of stone shot in every direction and pain sliced the exposed skin of her arms and hands when she threw them up to protect her face.

Air whooshed from her lungs when she landed on the ground, and a blast of searing heat hit her square on, her chest burning from the inside out.

Then everything went black.

****

When she came to, Livy found she'd collapsed at the base of the angel statue's pedestal. She sat up, wincing when pain sliced through her chest. Placing a hand over her heart, she frowned when confusion settled in. There was no visible wound. She held her arms up. She should see scratches from the shards marring her skin, but again, nothing was there.

A voice called to her from a distance.

"Miss? Are you all right?"

It was the elderly man who'd sent her to this section of the cemetery. It took him seconds to reach her, and when he reached down to help her to her feet, everything moved in slow motion. Livy's eyes shot back to the statue and widened when she saw it was back in perfect condition, just like the first time she'd laid her hands on it.

The angel's head and shoulders were still covered in green moss, and the tip of one wing was still chipped; the other still cracked. The only difference was now the pedestal contained some writing. The old man led her back toward the gate, but when she realized writing had shown up on the formerly blank spot, she struggled free of his grip to read the stone.

She saw only one word: SARAQVEL

The old man's gasp drew her attention. He, too, looked at the word on the stone.

"It can't be," he muttered absently.

"It can't be what?" Livy asked, but he didn't answer. He merely continued to stare at the writing for several long moments. She reached out to touch him, but he flinched before she made contact. With his eyes widened in horror, he backed away from the statue as if he'd seen a ghost.

"We have to go," he rasped, and his eyes zeroed to Livy's. "*You* have to go."

She didn't get the chance to ask anything else before he grabbed her arm in a deceivingly strong grip and that odd burst of warmth flooded her body again. She pushed the feeling aside as he led her back toward the gate. Her legs were numb from shock, so at first, he only managed to tug her, but when he glanced back at her, he cursed under his breath and turned to scoop her into his arms.

At first, he appeared deceivingly strong for such an old man, but then the dizziness hit her once again. Her head bobbed as her body started to relax and it was like she'd been given a huge muscle relaxer. She concentrated hard enough to look up at the man and his face wavered like a mirage. One moment he was old, wrinkled, and in the next, his skin was as smooth as hers. His stringy gray hair burst into a shiny golden blond and when he looked down at her, two of the bluest eyes she'd ever seen narrowed slightly.

"Sleep," he murmured, and for the second time today, darkness overcame her.

Chapter 2

The first thing Livy noticed upon waking up was the soft mattress beneath her and the pillow cradling her head like a huge marshmallow. Without opening her eyes, she knew the sunlight illuminating her eyelids was streaming in from her bedroom window. The familiar smell of the lavender fabric softener her mom used wafted from the comforter cocooning her.

"What a crazy dream," she grumbled and pulled the comforter over her head until she was a burrito. It took a few moments before she was fully awake. However, once she was, she remembered that her mom and dad were gone, dead and buried at Bonaventure Cemetery.

Upon remembering the funeral and graveside service, she jerked straight up in her queen-sized bed. What had happened afterward? Memories of an exploding statue, balls of fire soaring overhead, and an old man—who wasn't an old man at all—carrying her from the cemetery flashed through her mind.

But she couldn't remember how she got home.

Running her fingers through the spiky tufts atop her head, she threw her feet over the side of the bed and stood. Her entire body ached, but she didn't know why. She felt as though she'd been in a car crash. She decided she needed a long, hot shower, so she put one foot in front of the other and shuffled past her antique dresser to the bathroom, where she indulged herself. Afterward, she ambled across the small space, to the large mirror hanging over the sink, frowning when she realized it was completely fogged over.

She swiped a clean spot large enough to see herself and sighed at the dark bags under her eyes.

"More like luggage," she murmured and went about brushing her hair and teeth. She wasn't in a hurry, although her parents' lawyer asked to meet with her around three that afternoon and a glance at the clock hanging above the mirror said it was only eight. She had plenty of time to do…nothing.

A renewed sense of loneliness overwhelmed her. She didn't have anyone to have breakfast with or describe her crazy dream for. She was completely alone. It was then she decided she'd never fall in love and would certainly never marry. She couldn't bear to lose someone else. She wouldn't survive it. The pain was so palpable, like a weight crushing her chest. Her heart was broken, and she'd been told that only time would somewhat heal the wound. She couldn't and *wouldn't* love anyone else.

There was no reason for her to stay on in Savannah. She and her parents had taken her winter college break to move here, so she could start her new classes in January at the Armstrong Campus of Georgia Southern University.

She remembered the day just two weeks ago when they'd turned onto their street, and she noticed the sign boasting their street name.

"Lois Lane?" She'd snickered and met her dad's eyes in the rearview mirror from the back seat. "Really?"

Both her parents had laughed.

"At least it won't be hard to remember," her mom added, and then they'd all laughed.

Now, staring at the girl in the mirror, she wondered if she should stay here or move on to somewhere else, someplace that wasn't soiled with memories of a life she'd no longer have.

With thoughts of relocating on her mind, she dressed in her favorite jeans, which were, of course, ripped at both knees, and a black AC/DC T-shirt. She'd worn them both so often, the fabric was soft and somewhat comforting. Running a wide comb through her brown strands, she tamed them into some semblance of a hairdo and then headed downstairs for some breakfast.

About midway down the stairs, a loud knock on the front door caused her to falter slightly. She grabbed the wooden banister to keep herself from tumbling head over heels to the bottom.

With furrowed brows, she went to answer the door. She grabbed the brass knob and then stopped short of turning it. Her father had chided her too many times for answering the door without using the little peephole. He'd claimed she was too trusting when it never occurred to her that an ax murderer would knock.

Lifting to her tiptoes and squinting one eye, she peered through the hole with the other. An unusually tall blond-headed guy, about her age, stood on her front porch with a goofy smile on his handsome face.

"Must be lost," she murmured and shook her head. He shifted from one foot to the other, then ran his fingers through his unruly strands. He looked back at the door and raised his hand to knock again. It was like he expected someone he knew to answer it.

She grabbed the knob once more and, since it wasn't locked, gently eased the door open a tiny fraction. When her eyes met his, she gasped. He had the bluest eyes she'd ever seen, bluer than the sky *or* ocean. They were so blue they almost appeared turquoise. Suddenly, she felt like she'd seen those eyes before, and when she realized she was staring at him, she tore her gaze from them to study the rest of the mystery guy. He was kind of lanky, but judging by his healthy biceps, he carried enough upper-body muscle to be strong. He wore his collar-length blond hair shaggy like one would expect on a surfer. A soft sheen of peach fuzz covered his lower cheeks and jaw, and his full lips curved in a lopsided grin.

Her first thought was that there wasn't anywhere to surf in Georgia and her next was, holy cow, this guy was cute!

"Hi," he said, and she jumped. "Oh, sorry to startle you," he quickly apologized and chuckled. When she merely continued to stare, he shoved his hands into his jeans' pockets. He shifted his feet, and she glanced down, noticing that he wore a pair of black and white athletic shoes.

A cute surfer guy with good taste. Cute, but not her choice of dating material. She mentally scolded herself for even considering dating. What was she thinking?

"I just moved in next door." He pointed to the bungalow to the right of her house, and she leaned out far enough to look at the front of the house in question. "I've introduced myself to everyone else on the street but must've missed you yesterday," he explained, and she turned back to face him.

"I was at a funeral," she blurted and immediately wanted to slap a hand over her mouth. Where she'd been wasn't any of this stranger's business, and yet she felt the need to tell him everything about her and her life, which was kind of a stupid thing to do, just in case he was an ax murderer. Cute-surfer-guy-next-door may be his disguise. What girl wouldn't open the door to a good-looking guy like him?

She shook her head at the ludicrous thoughts rattling through her mind. It was bad enough that she grieved for her family. Now she added paranoid *and* schizophrenic to the mix. At this rate, she'd end up in an infirmary for the mentally insane before she turned twenty-one.

He pulled his right hand from his pocket and awkwardly shoved it in her direction. He had long, slender fingers perfectly suited for piano playing. *Was he a musician?*

He cleared his throat, and her eyes snapped back to his. He nodded down at his still outstretched hand and wiggled his eyebrows playfully.

Great, now he probably thought the girl next door was touched in the head.

Heat blossomed across her cheeks, and she mentally scolded herself for acting so weird. She wasn't exactly a social butterfly, but she also wasn't a shut-in. Her mom had taught her some manners and mediocre social skills, not that she'd displayed any so far this morning. All she'd done was ogle her new neighbor.

"I'm sorry," she said and reached to take his hand. The moment their skin touched, a strange rushing filled her ears, kind of like the time she'd visited Niagara Falls. The flowing water had been so loud that she couldn't hear her mom screaming at her to smile for the camera.

She jerked her hand from his and hastily wiped her palm against her jeans. He couldn't help but notice her action because he quickly shoved his hand back into his pocket.

"Sorry." He nodded at her hand. "My palms sweat when I'm nervous," he explained, and a beautiful pink blush warmed his cheeks. She opened her mouth to, no doubt, say something else stupid when a lock of blond hair gently slid across his forehead, and the ends landed directly in his eye. He tossed his chin, throwing the sprig back atop his head where it then stood in disarray like the rest.

"I'm Penn," he added, catching her wondering what kind of hair gel he used because that stuff was potent.

"Livy," she responded. "Actually, it's Olivia, but my parents call me Livy." She remembered their absence, and before thinking better she added, "They *used* to call me Livy."

His brows furrowed slightly in confusion, but he didn't say anything. She didn't want to explain herself but felt the need since she was the one who mentioned it.

"My parents died four days ago. I buried them yesterday." Just uttering the words left a sour taste in her mouth, and she swallowed hard to keep from vomiting on this cute boy's shoes.

He tucked his head and murmured his sympathies, but honestly, she was tired of hearing how sorry people were for her. She just wanted to pick up the shattered pieces of her life and move on, if that was even possible.

He shuffled his feet again, and she felt like a heel for wanting him to just go away. She just wanted to be left alone. Her thoughts were chaotic, and she was unable to focus on anything for longer than a second. Mentally, she wasn't in any shape to do anything other than lie on the sofa and drool.

He cleared his throat and lifted his eyes to hers, and again she was struck by how blue they were. Blue enough that she wanted to fall into them and live forever. She shook her head, again startled by the feelings swirling around inside of her.

"So sorry to bother you," he said and turned to descend the steps leading to the little flagstone walkway. She watched him until he reached the white picket gate and beyond. Once he passed through the gate, he closed it behind him and started down the sidewalk toward his house. Just before he reached the edge of his yard, he raised his hand and waved.

"It was nice to meet you," he called and hurried on out of view.

Without responding, she stepped back inside and let the door shut gently. She couldn't help but feel as though she'd met the guy before but knew it wasn't possible. She'd only been to a few places in town since they'd moved here, and that was counting the quick trip to Georgia Southern campus for some paperwork.

Shrugging off the sense of déjà-vu, she headed to the kitchen. Maybe she saw him walking around on campus or something. She would ask him should she run into him again.

****

Once out of sight, Penn rushed up the steps and

through the oak door of his little house.

Sem's waiting for an update, the voice in his mind said.

I'm on my way, he huffed. *Tell him to keep his shirt on.*

Since he worked with a group of ex-soldiers, Penn was used to their leader being edgy and even outrageous at times. The Grigori Watchers, the society he worked for, had been on Earth since Adam and Eve.

Penn was here on a critical mission, and his superior expected regular updates.

Directly inside the kitchen doorway to the left was another door that led to the basement. He shoved through the partially open door and clumped down the wooden stairs to the temperature-controlled room below.

A row of computer monitors lined three walls. One wall was nothing but your basic computers and monitors, which he utilized for property surveillance and climate change alerts. Another was lined with screens showing everything from national news to the Cooking Channel.

The soft whirring of fans cut the silence. He flicked a glance at each screen, and, satisfied with what he saw, he then turned and plopped down in a cushioned desk chair directly before the largest screen mounted on the wall just behind the stairs. He tapped a few keys on the keyboard, and a scowling face immediately filled the monitor.

His first thought was that Sem wore his anger well. The man's jet-black hair was cut in a wild—orange this time—mohawk, and multiple piercings adorned his eyebrows, nostrils, and lip. And when he narrowed his eyes, the black eyeliner lining his unusually green eyes made the scar notching his right eyebrow even more noticeable.

His second thought was interrupted by Sem. "Well?" the other man demanded. "Is she the one?"

Penn sighed heavily, his mind drifting back to the little episode in the cemetery yesterday. He couldn't explain the emotions that had suddenly burst to life within him when he'd taken Livy in his arms. He'd never felt that way before and certainly had never expected to feel it at all. He'd thought himself in love once, but the feelings were nothing like what he experienced when he'd touched Livy or taken her in his arms.

"Yes," he answered succinctly. "She is. She freed Saraquel yesterday."

Sem inhaled sharply. "Fuck me. How did she do it? She doesn't have the ring or the grimoire, right?" he asked. "How the *hell* did she do it?"

Penn shook his head, his own questions swirling within his mind. It hadn't made sense. According to all his research, only the combined powers of the Keeper, Solomon's signet ring, and the grimoire would break the lock, but he'd witnessed it with his own eyes. Livy hadn't had a book or a ring on any finger. Her hands were tiny and bare.

"I don't know. One minute Livy stood there studying the statue, and the next, she reached out and touched Sara's ring. Livy's body faded to that of a television station experiencing static—she looked like a Shade, Sem—and then a bright blue aura enveloped her, and she fell to the ground, unconscious." Penn recounted the scene. He'd also seen the balls of fire streaking through the sky, and he'd felt the ground quake beneath their feet. But he knew it was the Horsemen, exerting their powers and desire for freedom. Mortals wouldn't be able to see or feel them just yet. They hadn't gained enough strength for that.

But Penn could, and as he'd witnessed Livy's distraught expression, he could tell she'd felt them too.

"Did you see Sara?" Sem asked, his voice husky with emotion. "Are you positive she's free?"

Penn nodded gently, knowing the turmoil his friend felt. Saraquel was one of them, a Grigori, and in addition, Sem's sister. In truth, all the Grigori were brethren and regarded each other as siblings. Semjaza and Saraquel were twins.

Sem nodded his head sagely and sat back in his chair. Penn didn't miss the slight misting in the man's eyes.

"How's Luna?" Penn asked.

"She and the Hellhound are fine," Sem ground out, his voice almost a growl of displeasure. "They've gone to Hell. Cerberus is missing, and they've gone looking for her."

"Wait, Cerberus is missing?" Penn voiced his disbelief. Cerberus had guarded the Gates of Hell ever since The Fall. She never took a vacation and never *went missing*. With the Four Horsemen vying for freedom, now was not the time for Cerberus to be gone. "What the hell, Sem? Who's guarding the gate?" Penn asked.

"Amon and the Hellhound, from what I understand." Sem narrowed his eyes. "I don't like that Luna was dragged into Kurbane's drama. She has duties here."

"Kurbane has claimed her. There's nothing we can do about that," Penn argued. "Just keep an eye on Zeke," he warned. "You know how he gets." Zeke thought of Luna as a daughter and was overly protective of her. Penn wondered how many times Zeke had tried to kill Kurbane. It was a good thing he was a Hellhound. He'd survive most anything Zeke did to him.

"Sara hasn't called me," Sem mused softly, confirming Penn's assumption. "But as soon as she does, we'll bring her in. Michael is probably already aware of her escape. Watch your back," he warned Penn.

"I've got this," Penn said. "How should I proceed with Olivia?"

"Does she know anything?" Sem asked.

Penn shook his head. After rendering her unconscious, he'd gently probed her memories, shocked to realize she was ignorant of her true destiny. She had no idea who she was or what power she wielded.

"No," he answered simply. "I read her memories. Not even her mother knew, or if she did, she never mentioned it to Livy."

Sem nodded, his face tight and pensive, his brain no doubt hopping into overdrive.

"Stand by," Sem finally ordered. "Don't let her out of your sight. I'll be in touch," he added.

"I'll need more serum," Penn informed him. "I used the only one you sent with me yesterday."

Sem chuckled and clucked his tongue, obviously finding humor in his friend's discomfort.

"Why can't you just be your regular, charming self?" he asked, his fathomless green eyes twinkling with mischief.

"I did. She didn't like me." Penn frowned in response. Of all his team, he was the one with the most social skills, but that didn't mean he was entirely comfortable mingling with humans. Using one of Sem's potions to Shadow himself was much easier. He could take the form of anyone.

"She's very skittish and reclusive. All the neighbors say she's anti-social. How do you suggest I handle this without Shadowing myself? She's going to think I'm a stalker," he complained.

"Just watch from a distance," Sem advised. "Don't act all weird, and you should be fine. I'll be in touch soon," he confirmed, and then the screen went black.

I don't understand why we can't just maintain mental contact. Penn complained. *It would be much easier. Sem could hear and see everything I do and not have to wait for me to report in.*

Others can listen in. You know that, the voice responded. *Sem doesn't want to take that chance.*

"Fine," Penn muttered and pushed away from the computer. Wandering back upstairs, he sauntered into the kitchen and grabbed a soda from the fridge.

Taking orders was one of Penn's finest abilities, and manipulating technology was another. Being the voice of reason for Sem was his third and most honed. Yet, after all this time, he'd learned to trust Sem and his decisions, even when they didn't make sense, which was often.

He carried the cold can of soda with him to the sink, popped the top, and took a long pull of the citrus-flavored liquid. He involuntarily shuddered the moment the vile carbonated fluid hit his tongue, burning his soft tissue to the pit of his stomach. No matter how long he'd been on earth, he still hadn't developed a taste for junk food or the acid-infused, erosion-causing drinks called soda.

He shuddered when he thought about how bad the concoction was eating away his stomach lining.

"Hopefully, this mission won't last much longer," he murmured and promised himself an all-vegan diet, especially when he thought about all the refined sugars and empty carbs he'd recently inhaled.

Tossing back the can, he finished off the nasty drink and pitched the empty container in the trash before turning back to the little window over the kitchen sink. Although a tall, wooden fence divided his property from Livy's, her house was quite a bit larger than his, and it stretched out into her backyard just enough for Penn to catch a glimpse of her as she moved through the kitchen.

When Sem first gave him marching orders for this mission, he'd whined like a schoolgirl at bedtime. He hadn't wanted to come to Georgia. He was perfectly fine at HQ, but the boss-man wouldn't take no for an answer. Everyone else prepared for the impending war, and Penn was stuck babysitting. He didn't like it, but he followed orders like any good soldier.

After meeting Livy yesterday, he suddenly found himself pleased. He couldn't exactly explain the feeling that zapped his system today when they'd shaken hands but recognized it as the sign it was.

He was exactly where he was meant to be. The fact that he found her utterly adorable and was attracted to her was beside the point. He'd do his duty without falling for her.

He protected the world's greatest asset in the new war. He couldn't afford to get personally involved. That would only complicate things. Besides, he'd sworn off love forever.

Chapter 3

Livy shifted in the soft leather chair and tried her best to pay attention to the man reading her parents' last wishes. She'd tuned his voice out but still watched his lips move as he read the document. In her mind, it was all simple enough. Her parents had named her their sole heir and she'd received ownership of everything in their sizeable estate. The attorney had gone into the spiel, listing all her new acquisitions, but she tuned out his voice. She didn't care how much money she now had or how many homes she now owned. She'd have gladly given it all up for just one more day with her parents.

They gave up everything to move here with her. Her mother had sold her landscaping business and her father left the law firm where he'd been a partner for almost twenty-five years. They'd said goodbye to friends, their church, and neighbors, uprooted themselves, and moved across the country just because she wanted to attend Georgia Southern for her doctorate program.

Thinking back now, she felt so ashamed. She'd wanted to move here, but she didn't want to move alone. She wanted them with her. And it was because of her that they were now dead. If she hadn't insisted they *all* relocate, they would still be back home in Washington State, alive and well. She remembered the last time she'd seen them, talked to them.

"Dad and I are heading to the store. Is there anything you need?" Livy's mother had stood in her open bedroom doorway and smiled. Her brown hair was all sleek and shiny, always perfect, with not a strand out of place.

"No," Livy responded. "Just hurry back. We have outfits to put together."

Her mother smiled and blew her a kiss before muttering, "May the angels continue to watch over you."

Her mother's last words. Three miles from the local supermarket, an epileptic driver had a seizure and hit her parents head-on. No one had survived, and Livy's whole world turned upside down in the blink of an eye.

"Olivia?"

Her thoughts disappeared, and she looked up into Mr. Aston's eyes. She hadn't heard a word he'd said since he opened the will and began reading. She had no idea what he was waiting for.

"I'm sorry. I thought I was up for this today, but I don't think I am," she explained and gathered her purse. She rose from her chair to stand before his desk. "Can we reschedule?"

He frowned but shook his head.

"There's no reason to do that. You're the sole heir and everything you need to know is right here in this file, what bills they had, the bank accounts and such," he explained and handed her a large, at least four-inch-thick, black folder. She accepted it and looked back at him, with so many questions, but no order.

"You'll be fine," he said as his secretary arrived and gently rushed Livy out of his office. At first, she was shocked that he'd simply brushed her off, but grateful because now she could go home and read everything when she was ready.

She walked out into the small parking lot and got in her 2014 sports convertible, her high school graduation gift from her parents. She drove home in a fog of grief, shock, disbelief, and confusion. She'd contacted the college and postponed her classes until the fall semester. There was no way she'd be able to focus on anything until she'd mourned and finally accepted her new place in life.

It was strange to think that just a week ago, she'd had her entire future planned out.

Unlocking the front door, she stepped across the threshold into the empty, quiet living room. A slight breeze wafted in, sending dust motes scattering in the air. The sun's rays cut several streams through the slanted mini-blinds, illuminating the sparse furniture and lack of décor. Livy let her eyes roam over the room and realized just how empty her home was.

Suddenly tears overwhelmed her. She crumbled to the floor in a sobbing heap. Years of memories flashed through her mind, a timeline tidal wave, flipping through event after event, the process only widening the hole in her soul. She reminded herself to breathe, to keep breathing. She felt lost, abandoned, and untethered from everything and everyone.

"What am I going to do?" she whispered into the empty air. "I'm just a kid. I can't do this." Burrowing her face in her hands, she allowed the sobs to wrack her entire body until not an ounce of liquid remained. Her swollen eyes stung like they'd been scrubbed with sandpaper.

She lost track of how long she sat in the open doorway, the cool, brisk December wind gently sweeping across her. Moving from Washington to Georgia had been a contrast. Whereas Washington was enjoying snow flurries, the southern state's warmer climate surprised her with its multi-colored fall leaves still clinging to the trees like a last-ditch effort to remain alive.

It wasn't until a tall shadow loomed behind her, casting its silhouette across the wooden floor beneath her, that she realized she had started to shiver and was no longer alone.

"Are you all right?" a male voice asked. Its soft, soothing tones managed to calm her raw emotions. Penn stood on her porch, his face drawn in a pensive mask of concern, and she offered a small smile.

"Did you fall?" he added and indicated the floor. His eyes bore into hers. He could not help but see her red, swollen eyes. From the way he shifted his weight from one foot to the other told her he was uncomfortable and probably at a loss as to what to say or do next. The soft, understanding way he studied her said that he knew she'd been crying but decided to grant her a modicum of dignity.

Livy sniffled and used the hem of her T-shirt to dry her tear-streaked face. Pushing herself to stand, she turned to face him, doing her best to keep her small smile. Even though her heart ached, and dread filled her nerves, she did her best to appear normal, to offer some of the southern hospitality she'd read so much about.

"Hi, Penn," she greeted him.

"I didn't mean to bother you," he announced and took a step backward. "I just wanted to make sure you were all right." Then he turned and headed back down the walkway. Suddenly Livy didn't want to be alone. She wanted someone to sit and talk with her. She needed someone to remind her that life goes on. She didn't know anyone else in town, and her best chance was about to walk away.

"Wait," she called, gasping softly when he froze in his steps. Considering that he may not want to hang out with her, Livy steeled herself for the rejection. "Do you want to come in?"

When he turned toward her, his face lit with interest, his smile akin to the sunshine's warm rays. That one small gesture was enough to give her strength.

"I could use some company," she admitted sheepishly. "You seem like you're about my age. Would you like to hang out, maybe?" she asked and then admonished herself for rambling.

"I'd like that," Penn answered and moved back toward her. He paused at the threshold and simply peered down at her, and Livy swallowed the heavy lump that formed in her throat.

He was tall, much taller than she'd originally thought, and his bright, blue eyes peered down at her. Suddenly feeling self-conscious under his scrutinizing gaze, she reached up and fidgeted with the diamond stud in her right ear.

After merely standing and staring at each other in uncomfortable silence, Livy realized she had blocked the doorway. She emitted a nervous laugh and moved aside, gesturing for him to come in. He just continued to smile and brushed past her to stand in the middle of the living room.

Boxes were stacked haphazardly around the living

room, and Livy cringed at the untidiness. They were still in the process of unpacking from their cross-country move, a chore that was now up to Livy should she decide to stay.

"We just moved in," she offered lamely and motioned at the cream-colored sofa. "Please, sit down. Would you like a soda or some water?" she said.

"I'm good, thank you," he answered. "Where did you move from?" he added conversationally, and her heart lifted at his effort to launch into a normal conversation.

"Davis Falls, Washington," she answered. "It's a beautiful little town not far from the Oregon state line."

"So, what prompted you to move so far away?" he asked and folded his long, lithe form to sit on the sofa.

"School," Livy supplied easily enough and flopped down into the matching wingback chair. "I'm transferring to Georgia Southern…" Her voice trailed off as she suddenly wondered if she even wanted to finish her degree. "I, ah—" She cleared her throat and smiled. "I delayed my classes until next semester."

Penn nodded, the action causing him to appear older and wiser than a typical boy his age.

"Probably a good decision," he agreed. "But then again, you may want the distraction."

Livy frowned. She hadn't thought about it like that. Lifting her eyes back to his, the walls suddenly closed in on her, and she shifted uncomfortably. Her heart squeezed, and her airways tightened, signaling an oncoming anxiety attack, something she hadn't suffered in a few years, but she remembered the symptoms well.

Her breath grew labored, her eyes darting around the room as if she were watching shadows dance around in her periphery, and she was trying to pinpoint them. Her gaze lit on Penn, and he narrowed his eyes.

"Livy?" he murmured and sat forward on the sofa seat. "Are you all right?"

Instead of answering, Livy frantically shook her head and surged to her feet. A light sheen of sweat broke out on her forehead, and she raised trembling hands to twist the small diamond in her ear lobe.

"Can't breathe," she rasped and wrapped her arms around her waist.

Penn pushed off his seat and took her by the upper arms. He pushed her back into the wide-winged chair. He acted like he knew she was having an anxiety attack and was taking over the situation.

"Sit down," he instructed, and with his large hand gently cupping the back of her head, he guided her until she was bent forward, her face between her knees. "Slow your breathing, long breath in and hold, and then long breath out." His voice sounded like it came from the opposite end of a long tunnel. It rang deep and echoed throughout her mind.

Moving to her side, he ran his hand up and down the expanse of her back, using long, comforting strokes until her shoulders relaxed, and her gasps slowed to even pants.

"I'm so sorry," Livy murmured. Her words came out jumbled because her face was still stuffed between her knees. "It's been a long time since I've had an attack this bad. Usually, I can control them with my breathing."

Did she look like a total lunatic? She'd just met this guy yesterday and invited him into her home on a whim today because she didn't want to be alone. Now, she sat doubled over, her face virtually in her crotch, because she'd lost it. She was pathetic.

"No worries," he murmured, and she jolted at realizing his voice was much closer than she thought.

She brought her head up, intent on reclaiming as much dignity as she could, and the back of her head smacked a hard surface. A burst of stars clouded her vision.

"Oh, God." She lunged to her feet when she saw that she'd knocked him over with her quick movement. "I'm so, so sorry. Let me help you up."

Reaching forward, she managed to step on an upturned corner of the throw rug and lost her balance. She stumbled right into his lap. Heat scalded her face. Tears welled in her eyes, and she slowly lifted her face to apologize again. But when she took in his intense blue eyes, she forgot everything but the thought of again swimming in those luminescent pools. They were simply breathtaking and something someone could get lost in for hours on end.

Then he smiled, her heart jolted, and something shifted inside of her. Something she'd never felt before, a sense of longing for acceptance and peace. But more than anything, it was the desire for belonging. She'd always felt like an outsider, even within her hometown, and in truth, that was the reason she chose a college out of state.

"Are you okay?" he asked, and she didn't miss the twinkle of a smile in his eyes. Had he pulled her into his lap on purpose?

Clearing her throat, she untangled her arms and legs from his and rose to her feet, offering him her hand. "I'm better now, thanks."

He returned her smile and grabbed her hand, hauling himself effortlessly to his feet without so much as a tug from her.

Nervous energy filled Livy, and she bounced from foot to foot, her eyes darting everywhere but at the perfect guy in the room. He turned from studying her and looked beyond the living room area into the kitchen and dining room. She glanced at all the unpacked boxes and clutter and winced. She opened her mouth to again mumble excuses for her unkempt home but stopped short when he turned from her and headed toward the rooms in question.

She trailed after him, panic clogging her throat, her instincts demanding that she stop him from going any farther into her home, but he tilted his head as if listening to a sound she couldn't hear, and she backed off, curious as to where he thought he was going.

He crossed the threshold into the kitchen but didn't spare a glance at the dining room to the left. He moved straight through the room and out the double French doors to the generous backyard beyond.

Livy stopped dead in her tracks. She hadn't ventured past the doors since her parents died. The large backyard had been the selling point of the house as far as her mom had been concerned.

He looked back at her and smiled. "Someone had big plans. There must be two hundred plants out here."

Livy swallowed the lump in her throat and forced herself to follow him. Trepidation grew with every step she took through the kitchen, and once she reached the French doors, sweat beaded across her upper lip. A feeling of sickness balled in her stomach, but she made the steps that took her out.

She gasped when she took in all the potted plants: flowers, shrubs, fruit trees, and other various flora littered the entire backyard. Her mother had set them according to where she would plant them, and it was beautiful.

"She never got the chance to put them in the ground," Livy murmured, her eyes misted, and her sight blurred. "I didn't even know she'd bought them."

Penn placed his hand on her shoulder, and she took some comfort from his warmth. She couldn't believe she'd ignored the area; all those beautiful plants would have died had Penn not invaded. She realized that she owed him.

She tilted her head back and looked up at his eyes. "Thank you for showing this to me. I would never have stepped foot out here on my own."

He smiled back at her and winked. "We have lots of work to do. How about we start first thing in the morning?"

Livy inhaled sharply. "You want to help me plant them?" she asked. "Why?" She didn't mean to sound so suspicious, but in her experience, people didn't take so much work upon themselves unless they had something to gain.

"It's the perfect way to spend more time with you," he said.

Livy smiled. His honesty was just one thing she liked about him.

"All right. In the morning," she responded. "What time?"

"What time do you normally get up?" Penn smirked.

****

After saying goodnight to Livy, Penn returned home and immediately headed to his basement. Sem and Zeke had been strangely quiet during Penn's entire visit with Livy, and Penn was slightly worried. It wasn't like either one to disappear during a job.

Penn sat down and started typing on his keyboard. He sent Sem a text. Fifteen minutes went by with no response, so he shot Zeke a text.

—*What's up?*— Zeke responded almost immediately.

—*Where's Sem? Call me or get your feathered butt here for a debrief. I have news.*— Penn responded.

Within seconds, the air around Penn thickened, an outline of a person shimmered, and the seven-foot-two-inch-tall man with scars covering every square inch of his face materialized.

He wore head-to-toe black: from his dark, spiked hair, fingerless leather gloves, and long leather duster, to his leather pants, T-shirt, and biker boots. He looked like a motorcycle-riding badass. If anyone met him in a dark alley, they would think him a monster from Hell, and then they would run.

Zeke stroked his dark goatee and looked around the basement. His eyes finally settled on Penn.

"I'm here. What's the update?"

"This is going to take longer than I thought," Penn said. "She has no idea who she is, and I have no idea how to tell her. She suffers from severe anxiety, and I can't just blurt it out during a conversation. I need to know how to proceed. She and I are going to start gardening tomorrow, so I'll get to spend more time with her. I hope we'll form a friendship. That would make it easier to tell her. What do you think?" Penn clamped his lips shut and ran fingers through his blond, floppy hair. "Help?"

Zeke's black eyes widened. "Well, I'd say you're on the right track. Just keep doing what you're doing. I'll brief Sem, and I'm sure he'll be in touch." Then he dematerialized and was gone.

"Wait!" Penn called. "Where's Sem?"

Sem is with his sister. He knows you have an update and will be in touch soon. The voice rolled through his mind. Penn sat back, crossed his arms, and scowled.

"He better."

Chapter 4

Livy awoke to the sun streaming in through her parted curtains. She stretched and smiled. She was looking forward to spending time with Penn. He was thoughtful, considerate, and gorgeous. She also liked the way she felt when he was around. It wasn't exactly peace, but maybe a sort of serenity, as if all her worries were nothing but dust motes floating in the air. He'd also reminded her that her worries and stress couldn't harm her unless she let them, and that was something she was going to work on. She was tired of letting things control her.

She bounced from the bed and dressed in an old pair of jeans and a Motley Crew T-shirt. She raced down the stairs, strode into the kitchen, and opened the fridge. She was famished. She pulled a couple of eggs from the carton and cooked them, eating them while she stood at the counter. She put her plate in the sink and started for the door.

She opened the door to look for the morning paper and gasped when she came face-to-face with Penn.

"Wow, I was just thinking about you," she said and smiled. Stepping back, she motioned for him to come in. "Hope you're ready for some work," she added and closed the door behind him. Like yesterday, she followed him out into the backyard.

"I'll take the big flower bed over by the fence.

What are you going to tackle?" Penn pointed to their left at where her mother had placed gallon buckets of daylilies, Easter lilies, lily of the valley, tiger lilies, and goldband lilies.

Livy surveyed the yard. The bed immediately to their left was a handful of hydrangea plants.

"I'll take these," she said and smiled.

"Might as well get to work." He nodded and set off to his corner.

They worked in comfortable silence for a few hours and then took a break for refreshments.

Before they could start a decent conversation, a head popped over the side fence.

"Hello there," he said. "How are y'all doing today? I just moved in and noticed y'all working. Need any help?"

Livy noticed Penn stiffen. She thought it was sweet how he wanted the two of them to be alone, or at least she hoped that's what he thought.

"Welcome to the neighborhood," Livy called back. "Thanks for the offer, but I think we've got it covered."

"Okay then, well, holler if you need anything," he called back. "By the way, my name is Jordan. What's yours?"

"I'm Livy, and this is Penn. He lives next door too."

"Nice to meet y'all," he said and then disappeared behind the fence.

Livy turned to Penn and frowned. "Are you okay?"

Penn looked at her and smiled his gorgeous smile.

"I'm fine. Shall we get back to work?"

****

Penn set his bottle of water down and headed back

to the lily bed he'd been working on. His heart hammered in his chest.

I have a problem, he called in his mind. *We have a demon sniffing around. What do I need to do?*

Can you vanquish it without attention?

No, not now.

Keep an eye on it, and keep us updated.

"Great," Penn muttered and stabbed the hand trowel into the loose soil.

"How's it going?" Livy called from where she knelt to the left of the back doors, working on a bed of red petunias. Penn glanced over his shoulder and smiled. She'd already tackled and completed the hydrangeas and then moved to the other side of the patio doors. She'd done a wonderful job of placing the plants. The dark mulch would make their color pop come spring.

"Going great. How about you?" he called back.

"Great!" she said, and they both went back to working in their companionable silence. They worked the rest of the day that way, each one lost to their task. Penn spent his time worrying about the demon next door. He needed to vanquish it, but he had to think about possible witnesses. Tonight, he'd sneak into the thing's house and send it back to Hell where it belonged.

"What do you say we call it a day?" Livy said, and Penn jumped, falling straight on his ass. He hadn't heard her approach him. He stood and groaned when his back twinged.

"If you're ready," Penn answered, turning to face her and rubbing at the painful spot. He looked around at where they'd both been working and nodded his head.

"I'd say we made some pretty good progress today, wouldn't you?" He looked down at her and smiled. He noticed a smudge of dirt on her cheek and, without thinking, reached out to brush at it.

Caught off-guard, Livy's eyes widened.

"Sorry," Penn said. "You have some dirt just here—" He pointed at his cheek.

"Oh." She laughed and reached up to wipe at it. "Thanks." They stood and simply stared at each other for several long seconds. Penn couldn't help noticing just how beautiful she was.

Her big, lime-green eyes sparkled in the afternoon sun. Her pixie-cut hair glistened in several different colors of brown and auburn. Penn found himself softening toward her. Her tongue darted out to wet her lips, and his body reacted in a way it hadn't for centuries. He couldn't remember the last time he'd had a woman. Of course, not just any woman would do. Penn wasn't one for casual dalliances. He was old-school—he had to have feelings for the woman before he took her to his bed.

His eyes moved back to hers, and he noticed that hers were narrowed thoughtfully.

"Are you listening to me?" she asked, and his eyes moved back to her lips—full and luscious, he imagined the way they'd feel pressed against his own. He shook his head to dispel the naughty thoughts and averted his attention back to her.

"I'm sorry. I was lost in thought," he said and smiled. "What were you saying?"

Livy laughed, and a light blush stole across her cheeks as if she'd known what he'd been thinking. Wishful thinking had him wishing she'd been thinking the same thing.

You seriously need to get laid, my friend. The voice brushed through his mind.

Mind your own business and stay out of my head! Penn sent back and remembered they needed to be in his head to know what was happening. He inwardly rolled his eyes.

"Would you like to join me for dinner?" Livy asked, and Penn met her eyes again. Those light-green pools could probably beckon him to do anything she desired.

"Um, yes," Penn accepted before any second thoughts reared their ugly heads. It was the perfect way to keep an eye on her. "That sounds great. Would you mind if I went home to shower and change?"

"Of course! I need to do the same and I'm cooking, so take your time," she added and turned to head to the back doors. Penn watched the sway of her hips and shook his head. He was in way over his head.

****

Livy raced through a quick shower and dressed in a light, flowery sundress that was perfect for the unseasonably warm December air. Running her fingers through her short hair, she called it styled. She'd never been one for makeup, but she applied some light brown eyeshadow and black mascara. Modeling in the mirror, she decided she was ready.

Heading downstairs, she left her feet bare and went to work in the kitchen. By the time the doorbell rang, she was taking lasagna and garlic bread out of the oven and had just turned the burner off under the green beans. She wiped her hands on her apron and pulled it off over her head. She tossed it through the laundry room doorway beside the dining room door and went to answer the door.

But it wasn't Penn on her porch, it was Jordan. He held out a bouquet of red roses and smiled.

"Hi again," he said. "I was wondering if you'd join me for dinner." Not waiting for an answer, he brushed past her to enter the house.

Livy's heart raced at the sudden intrusion of a stranger into her home. She turned to face the man, leaving the door open at her back, and hoping that Penn arrived soon.

"That's a nice gesture, but I already have plans," she answered and swept her arm toward the open door. She hoped he'd get the message and leave but instead, he turned to venture deeper into the house. Torn between standing by the safety of the open door and going after him, she chose to stand by the door.

He walked to the back door and looked out into her yard.

"Y'all got a good bit done today. You must be proud," he called over his shoulder. "Wish you'd accepted my offer to help." He turned back to face her across the house. "I could help you with a lot of things." He took a step toward her, and suddenly, the distance wasn't far enough. But Livy refused to flee her sanctuary. She would not run, no matter how threatened she felt.

But before Jordan took another step in her direction, he turned and fled through the back doors, and Penn ran past Livy after him. She closed the front door and locked it, then ran in Penn's wake.

She stopped at the open French doors and scanned the backyard. Penn stood in the open yard, scowling at the fence separating Jordan's property from Livy's.

"Where did he go?" she asked and threw her hands up.

"He scaled the fence," Penn answered and turned his attention back to her. "Are you all right? He didn't hurt you, did he?"

Livy shook her head.

"No, he didn't hurt me. He just scared me. I opened the door, and he practically shoved me out of the way to get inside my house. He wanted me to go to dinner with him. I think he's crazy," she finished and whirled her finger in the air beside her temple.

Penn came toward her, stopping to stand on the two brick steps below where she stood.

"I want to have dinner with you. Am I crazy?" He smiled that dazzling smile, and the butterflies in her stomach fluttered.

"Maybe a little," she teased and waved him inside. Suddenly she wanted all the doors closed. All thoughts of eating outside made her nauseous. She pulled the French doors closed and turned to see him bent over the lasagna.

"This smells delicious," he said with his eyes widened in awe. "I've never had homecooked lasagna before. It's always out of a box, and then I have to nuke it in that unholy box of radiation."

Livy laughed out loud. "I'm sorry, I've just never heard a microwave called that," she apologized. "Yes, it's homemade, my mom's recipe and so easy to make." She joined him at the counter and leaned over to sniff it. It did smell divine. Turning her face upward to look at him, she smiled broadly. "Although the green beans are out of a can. Hope that's alright."

"Let's eat," Penn announced with a grin on his face.

"Would you like to eat in the dining room or the breakfast nook?" she asked and pulled two plates from the cabinet.

She spooned a healthy portion of lasagna on Penn's plate, placed a couple of slices of garlic bread beside it, and finished it off by spooning some green beans in the space beside the bread.

"I could eat this standing up, so it's up to you," he teased and accepted the offered plate with a grin. He brought the plate to his nose for another sniff and hummed. "If this tastes half as good as it smells, I'll be in heaven."

"Prepare yourself for the trip," Livy teased and giggled. It felt good being lighthearted again. She motioned for him to follow her, and she led him around the open partition that housed the stove and oven, to the breakfast nook sitting just on the other side. They took their seats and tucked in.

It didn't take Penn long to clean his plate, and he sat back in the chair, patting his belly with a smile.

"That was delicious, Livy. I don't think I can eat another bite."

"Oh, I forgot dessert!" Livy scowled. "I do have some strawberry cheesecake in the fridge if you'd like something sweet," she said and scooted her chair back to stand. She mentally chastised herself for forgetting about the after-dinner treat. That just went to show that she was a hot mess. But Penn didn't seem to mind, so she wouldn't worry about it overmuch. She pulled the pie from the fridge and grabbed the pie server from the utensil drawer. She set them both on the small table between their plates and retook her seat.

Penn eyed the pie with a gluttonous smile. "Shall I cut it?" he asked, and his eyes twinkled.

"Be my guest." Livy chuckled and continued to eat her dinner. She wasn't big on dessert, which was probably why she hadn't thought about it to begin with. But she enjoyed watching Penn's excitement. He was like a kid in a candy store.

He sliced a piece and placed it on his plate.

"Did you make this too?" he asked and shoved a forkful in his mouth. He rolled his eyes heavenward and smiled.

"I'm afraid not," Livy answered. "One of our neighbors brought it over." She finished off her lasagna and green beans and sat back to watch him enjoy a large strawberry from the top of the pie. A twinge of sadness gripped her stomach. A week ago, she was enjoying dinner with her mom and dad. It just went to show how quickly someone's life could change. Hers had flipped upside down in the manner of seconds.

His voice brought her back to the here and now. "And you haven't tried it?" he asked, his eyes wide in shock. "It's delicious."

"I'm not real big on desserts. You can take it home with you if you like," Livy said. He nodded his head and smiled before taking another bite.

After he finished his dessert, Livy started gathering the plates and glasses from the table, only to have him take them from her.

"You cook, I'll clean," he said and headed to the sink with the dirty dishes. Livy hurried to trail behind him, objecting all the way.

"I'll just put them in the dishwasher." Livy flipped

the latch on the appliance and opened the door. She did back away and let Penn load the dishes. She handed him a soap pod and he closed the door, pushed the button for the correct setting, and it started up with a soft whir.

"See? I can be handy in the kitchen as well," Penn mused, and Livy laughed.

"Are you saying that you're housebroken?" she teased and punched him lightly on the arm. She watched a blush creep up his flawless skin and felt her own skin warm. Were they flirting? It had been so long since she'd been around a guy, she'd almost forgotten how to act.

"Well, it's getting late. Are you going to be okay tonight?" Penn asked and placed his hand on her shoulder. "I could stay, sleep on the sofa," he offered. But Livy refused.

"Well, at least let me give you my phone number." He smiled. "In case you have any more trouble."

"I'm sure he won't try anything tonight, if ever again," she said and offered him a pad of paper and a pen. "You chased him off, and if he does come around again, I'll call the police, but I appreciate the offer." She genuinely did appreciate him. He was helping her with the backyard, he helped her with the dishes, and he chased off a bad guy in her time of need.

He was beginning to grow on her.

Chapter 5

Livy double-checked the dishwasher and turned to survey the kitchen. Satisfied that it was clean, she tossed the dishtowel over the stove handle to dry and went to check the locks on the French doors and then the front door. She wouldn't admit it to Penn, but she was still shaken from Jordan's earlier invasion. He'd rattled her comfort in her own home, and that made her angry.

Penn had offered to stay the night with her and sleep on the sofa, but she didn't feel comfortable with that, so she'd sent him home with a to-go plate and a cheesecake with promises to continue their gardening tomorrow. Her back pinched just thinking about kneeling and hunching all day, but in the end, she enjoyed bringing her mother's vision to fruition.

Since she'd showered earlier, she pulled off her sundress and hung it back on the hanger in her closet and donned her pajama bottoms and tank top. She pulled back her comforter and crawled into the softness of her bed. She reached out to turn the bedside lamp off but stopped short when her eyes fell on the book sitting atop her table.

Christine Feehan's *Dark Prince* mocked her. She'd read the first half, but with everything that had happened, she hadn't picked it up in a while. She decided that she wasn't tired enough to sleep yet and pulled her bookmark out of page 368. Delving into the world of Romanian vampires, she didn't pay much attention when a limb scraped her window or thunder announced the bright light streaking through the sky. Nor did she notice when the wind picked up.

The storm was there before she knew what happened. The tree outside her window slammed against the glass panes with enough force Livy was afraid they'd shatter. She had a brief moment where she worried about the newly planted flowers but accepted there was nothing she could do about them now. She got up, intent on closing the shutters, but suddenly the power went out, and she was left in darkness. She felt her way back to the bed and again crawled between the sheets. Her parents had a generator in the shed out back, but she didn't know how to operate it. She considered calling Penn, but decided against it. It was nighttime, and she could go to sleep in the darkness. She wouldn't need any electricity until the morning. She pulled the covers up to her chin and lay back on her pillow.

A faint glow came from somewhere downstairs, and she almost panicked, but then she remembered the battery-operated light her dad had installed in the stairwell for power outages. Slightly comforted, Livy lay back and closed her eyes and tuned her ears into the raging storm outside.

She had just about dozed off when she heard a rustling sound from downstairs. She sat up, squinted into the partial darkness, and pulled the covers securely up to her chest. When something large hit the floor and shattered, Livy gave all pretenses of being brave and grabbed for her phone. She dialed Penn and retreated under the covers.

"Hello," he answered on the first ring.

"Penn? It's me, Livy," she said.

"Livy, are you okay?" he asked, his voice filled with concern.

"No," she breathed into the phone. "I think someone is in my house. Can you come over and have a look around?"

"Be right there." He hung up, and Livy curled into a ball.

Suddenly the covers were ripped from her body, and something grabbed her around the ankle. She screamed with every ounce of power she possessed, and thunder and lightning erupted through the sky and the entire house shook on its foundation. The beefy grip dragged her from her bed, her body hitting the floor hard enough to knock the breath from her lungs. She struggled for air, and she struggled to break free of the ironclad grasp.

She kicked with both legs, but the grip didn't lessen. Whoever had her was much stronger than she was. Somewhere amongst her panicking thoughts, she heard a pounding on the front door and remembered Penn couldn't get in.

"Penn," she screamed. "Help me! Bust out a window. Help!" She continued to struggle the best she could, but the man reached down and grabbed her other ankle and dragged her to him so quickly she couldn't do anything but collect splinters in her butt. The sound of broken glass meant that Penn had heard her, and he was coming in. She just hoped that between the two of them they could take the man.

"He won't help you now," the man growled in an unearthly voice. "You're mine."

"Like hell she is," Penn snarled and launched himself at the man's back. With Penn hammering on him from behind, the man had no choice but to let Livy go. The moment he did, she scampered to the far side of the room and sank to the floor. She was helpless in a fight, always had been.

She could only watch on in horror as the men grappled at each other, Penn finally getting his arms around the goon's neck, then flinging him across the room to crash into her antique dresser. The mirror hit the floor and splintered into a thousand pieces. Livy screamed. She couldn't help it. She was scared, and her anxiety had just shot through the roof.

The man punched Penn in the face, and Penn stumbled to his knees. With her heart hammering in her chest, Livy took the lamp from her bedside table and crept up on the man. She crushed the lamp against the man's skull, but he merely turned to face her, and she screamed again.

His eyes glowed red, a stark contrast to the darkness enveloping them. He advanced on her again, his mouth opening into a gaping maw, ragged teeth lining his wide lips.

"Oh my God," she screamed and backed away, cutting her feet on the broken glass. "What the hell are you?"

"Livy, get down!" Penn shouted, and a bright glow in the shape of a sword lit the room. Penn whipped the blade side-to-side and advanced on the man's back. Livy's eyes widened and she automatically dropped to her knees. This wasn't what she'd had in mind when she'd asked for help. They should be calling the police, not wielding a sword in her bedroom.

But before Livy could protest, Penn swung the glowing blade at the man's head and connected with a sickly sucking sound. Then the man exploded into a red mist and evaporated into thin air.

Livy screamed again.

****

Penn whipped the sword down to his side in a move meant to dispel blood from the blade. But as he'd just dispatched a demon, the sword was clean. He willed it back to nothingness and advanced on Livy, where she sat on the floor screaming. He offered his hand, but she was too hysterical to pay him much attention.

He knelt in front of her and offered her his open palms.

"Livy, listen to me. You need to stop screaming and listen to me. You're safe now." He talked gently and hoped he was getting through to her. He couldn't blame her hysteria. It wasn't every day that someone lopped off another person's head with a glowing sword. He was just glad he hadn't brandished his wings. That would have set her off.

"You killed him!" she managed to say between short breaths. "You killed him with a freaking sword. What kind of person does that? We need to call the police." She stood and started toward the bed where she'd left her phone. "*I* need to call the police."

Penn caught Livy's arm and pulled her to a stop. She whirled on him, snatching her arm from his grasp. He put his hands up again.

"Okay, okay, just calm down. You need to think about this." He swept his hand to encompass the room. "There's no body. The only sign of a break-in is the window I broke. What are you going to tell them?"

"*No* body?" Livy echoed and brushed past him to search the floor. She turned back to face him, her face a mirror of shock and confusion. "Where did he go?"

"Livy, I need you to sit down before you step on more glass," Penn said. "I'll explain everything. I promise." He reached out to take her arm, hesitant lest she jerked away again. She let him, and she let him guide her to the bed.

"Start talking," she demanded and sat down on the edge of her mattress.

"Okay, here goes nothing," Penn rasped and knelt to examine her dainty feet. "That thing was no man. It was a demon." He picked a foot up and hissed at the nasty cuts on the bottom. "You have a first aid kit? I need to bandage these cuts."

"In the bathroom, under the sink," Livy answered. "And what do you mean he was a demon? Demons only exist in books and stories. I know because I read a lot." She'd said the last like it made a difference.

Penn went into the bathroom and knelt in front of the sink. He rummaged through the cabinet until he found the kit and then returned to where she was still sitting. Well, she hadn't run away screaming, so that was a good sign that maybe she'd be accepting of the truth. They were running out of time.

"I'm not making this up. It was a demon, and it came to claim you for their side. There's a war brewing, and you have an important role in it. I was sent to help you find your way. We need some alcohol to clean the cuts," he mused and looked up into her face.

"Same place you found the kit," she said and frowned. "You sound like the fantasy book I've been reading. Demons aren't real, so what is really going on?"

Penn huffed and went to get the alcohol. He swiped a washcloth and returned to tend to her feet. As hysterical as she was from the ordeal, he couldn't believe her calm refusal of what he explained. He only knew of one way to prove it to her, and she was probably going to freak out, but what choice did he have? He'd already wasted enough time trying to ease into her life. Even though he'd enjoyed every minute they'd spent together, time was something he didn't have.

"What if I could prove it to you?" he asked and began cleaning the soles of her feet.

"How could you possibly prove it to me? You have another demon hiding in your pocket?"

Without a word, Penn spread his wings. The breadth of them filled the interior of her room.

Livy gasped and leaned away from him. He looked up into her face and sighed when she started breathing hard. Before she could do anything else, Penn shoved her head between her knees and patted her on the back.

"Just breathe," he coaxed. "It'll pass. Just long breath in and long breath out."

Penn continued bandaging her feet until her breathing had returned to normal. He'd left his wings out, knowing she wouldn't believe one glance. He'd just put the last wrap on when he felt her eyes on him. He lifted his head and stared into those beautiful green eyes.

"Do you believe me now?" he asked and arched his brow.

"Can I touch them?" she whispered with widened

eyes.

"Of course," Penn said and stopped tending her feet so that she could get up.

Livy rose from the bed, and ignoring the glass still littering the floor, she walked around behind him. She raised her hand and gently brushed a feather, and a tingling sensation rushed through Penn's body. It felt like she caressed his soul. He closed his eyes and allowed the feeling of her fingers playing along his feathers to wash over him, through him, into the very depths of his body, and his body reacted.

"How is this possible?" she asked, her voice soft and reverent, not at all panicky like before.

"You are just as special," he murmured and brought his wings in. He turned to face her and smiled. "You have a destiny far greater than mine."

"No," she said and crossed her arms. "This isn't happening. I'm dreaming. I'm having a nightmare, and I'm attracted to you, so it makes sense that you'd be in my dream."

"You're attracted to me?" Penn asked, and his heart skipped a beat. She'd thrown him completely off course with that one little word.

"Of course, I am. Who wouldn't be? You're gorgeous," Livy said and reclaimed her seat on the bed.

Penn's heart jumped at her confession. He wondered if she wanted him as much as he wanted her. She reached out and ran her finger along his jawline, and he almost lost his composure.

"And if this is a dream?" Penn asked softly and reached out to cup her face in his hand.

"Then I'd do this," Livy said and stood to face him. She ran her hand around his neck and pulled his face down to hers. She pressed a very soft kiss to his lips and then pressed her body closer to his.

Penn couldn't help it. He cupped her face in his hands and brought her lips back to his. He pressed his lips to hers again, but this time he parted her lips with his tongue and went all in. He lost himself in the kiss. He was flying, floating, walking on clouds, and it was like nothing he'd ever felt before.

He pulled away to see her face flushed with desire. She wanted him, and oh, did he want her. But he couldn't take advantage of her, not when so much had recently happened. He couldn't offer her the love she deserved. He *wouldn't* fall in love with her. Too much depended on him keeping his head and his heart straight, and she deserved more from a lover. Not to mention that she'd accepted that he was an angel too easily. By all rights, she should be hysterical.

He dropped his hands and took a step away, his gut twisting when she frowned at him, her arms still open where he'd been.

"We can't do this, Livy. We have things to do. You have a destiny to fulfill," Penn said. "There is a time and place for everything, and now is not it." He wanted her to understand why he turned her down. She needed to understand that it simply wasn't going to happen. Oh, he wanted her, so fiercely that it took everything in him to release her and step back.

"I understand," she finally murmured and dropped her arms. "I can't deny what I've seen with my own eyes. So, angels and demons are real. What is this 'destiny' you keep mentioning?"

"We'll talk about that soon. Right now, we need to get your room back to order and get this glass off the floor before you cut yourself any worse." Penn bent down and began picking up large pieces of the glass.

"I'll go get the broom and dustpan. We can use my trashcan over there." She pointed to the large wastebasket beside her nightstand.

"Be careful. Here. Use my phone as a flashlight." He pulled a smartphone from his pocket and tossed it to her. She caught it and went through the process of turning on the tiny light. Once it was shining, she turned and headed downstairs.

The demon is gone. Penn reported in. *It broke into her house and was dragging her away. I killed it in front of her. I also showed her my wings.*

Have you told her yet? the voice in his mind came back. *The Horsemen are chipping away at the Gates. We need her now.*

I'll tell her soon. At least let her rest for the night. She's been through a lot, and she's accepted the existence of things most humans would run and hide from.

You should stay with her, in case any more demons were dispatched to abduct her.

Penn flinched at the thought. He couldn't stay with her, could he? He'd offered earlier, but only out of courtesy. He knew she would turn him down. Now things were serious.

Only if she asks. I won't force myself upon her.

Whatever you wish. Just keep her safe. Right now, she's our only hope.

He heard Livy coming up the stairs and reached down to continue picking up shards of glass. He wanted nothing more than to curl up in her arms and forget the impending apocalypse, but that was impossible.

She started sweeping. They worked together until all the glass was off the floor, and Penn stood, stretching his back. He opened his mouth to tell her goodnight, but she stopped him.

"Would you stay the rest of the night with me? I know it's so girly of me, but I'm scared, and I feel safer with you here." She chewed on her lower lip and shifted her feet.

See? A brief chuckle swept through his mind, and he almost groaned.

"Of course. It's the least I can do," Penn agreed. "I'll take the sofa."

"No." Livy stopped him with a hand on his forearm. "You can sleep in the bed with me. I promise I won't bite. Please?"

She won't bite, the voice sing-songed.

Shut up and go to sleep, Penn shot back. He smiled at Livy and gave a curt nod. He didn't trust himself to speak. He waited for her to straighten the bed sheets and toss the blanket over the bed.

She crawled in first, and he pulled all the covers over her body and then lay down beside her.

"Will you hold me?" she asked in a voice so tender and soft that it nearly broke his heart. He wrapped his arms around her and snuggled his body close, close enough to comfort her and close enough to torture him.

"Better?" he asked, ignoring the hardening in his lower body. He had to get his mind on anything besides the sexy girl in his arms.

"Much better. Are you comfortable?"

I could die right now and be the happiest man on Earth.

Careful what you wish for, brother. You still have a

long road ahead of you.

Penn blocked out the voice and focused on the here and now. Holding Livy felt so right, like it was meant to be. He put that thought on the back burner and tried to play out what he would say to her in the morning. He needed a game plan. He had lots to tell her, and he hoped she would take it as well as everything else so far.

"Goodnight, Penn," Livy murmured.

"Goodnight, Livy, sweet dreams." Penn closed his eyes and ran through possible conversation starters. He finally felt her body relax and knew she'd fallen asleep. It wasn't that much later that he followed her into dreamland.

Chapter 6

Livy awoke to an empty bed and the smell of coffee in the air. She still couldn't believe that Penn had turned down easy sex last night. It wasn't like she was asking him to fall in love with her. She didn't want that. Maybe she needed to go about it differently. Her body wanted his, and she was pretty sure he'd wanted her.

She got up and grabbed her robe on the way downstairs. She entered the kitchen and stopped short at the sight of Penn hunched over her stove, wearing her mom's apron. Although the sight was a bit comical, the smell was divine.

"What are you cooking?" Livy asked and raised her nose to the air for another sniff. "It smells delicious."

Penn turned to face her, wielding a spatula and a gorgeous smile.

"A traditional Irish breakfast," he announced proudly. "We have bacon, sausage, baked beans, poached eggs, mushrooms, grilled tomatoes, and hash. I hope you're hungry." He turned back to the stove and continued pushing the mushrooms around in the skillet.

"Are you Irish?" Livy asked and took a seat at the bar facing the countertop stove. "You don't have an Irish accent," she pointed out.

"I'm not originally from Ireland, but I lived there for a long time before moving here for my job," he said and took a platter from the cabinet.

"Well, I see you've made yourself comfortable in my kitchen. Do you always cook?" Livy's heart warmed at the sight of him in her space. He handled himself like he knew what he was doing, and that was a major turn-on for her. She'd seen him do dishes; she was almost ready to marry him on the spot. No, that was a joke. She'd never marry. That dream was dead and gone. She did her best to forget about last night, about the fact that he had wings. She wasn't sure exactly what he was, and she hated to admit that she was afraid to ask. She didn't want to know. She didn't want anything to spoil the moment right now. Everything was perfect.

"Only when it's for someone who'll appreciate it," Penn answered and began stacking platters on his arms. "Shall we take this to the dining room?" he asked, and Livy nodded her head in agreement. She motioned to the open doorway and followed him into the dining room, where the large oak table sat. It hadn't seen much action since they'd moved in, and the thought of eating on it without her parents sent a pang through her chest.

Penn seemed to know what she was thinking, because he placed the platters strategically on the table and then put his hand on her shoulder.

"We can eat at the breakfast nook if you'd rather…" He trailed off, giving her time to make up her mind.

"No," she said. "You've gone through all this trouble. I want to enjoy it. This is the perfect place."

Penn nodded and pulled the chair out for her. She sat, then pulled it closer to the table.

"You stay right here. I'll be right back," he said

and scampered back into the kitchen. He returned with plates, forks, spoons, knives, and napkins. He set the table, taking extra care in placing the silverware in the correct positions by the plate. Finally, he took his seat at the head of the table and began spooning food onto his plate.

"You are too good to be true, Penn," Livy murmured.

"Dig in," he responded with a bright smile. "We've got a big day ahead of us."

Livy smiled back and loaded her plate. She had questions—so many questions—but she didn't want to ruin a perfect thing. She wanted them to go on like this forever, with no outside interruptions. But she knew that wasn't possible, that eventually, the other shoe would drop, and her perfect illusion would shatter. It always happened.

She made chit-chat while they ate and tried to draw out the moment as long as she could, but all too soon, they were done with their meal, and Penn began clearing the table.

"Here, let me help," Livy said and pushed her chair back. "You cooked. It's only fair that I clean." She repeated his words and reached out, taking a couple of empty platters, and followed him into the kitchen, where she placed the platters in the sink. Penn opened the dishwasher door and began loading it. Working together, it didn't take them long to get everything cleaned up.

"Are you ready for this?" Penn asked tentatively. "We have a lot to talk about."

"Can you start by telling me exactly what you are?" she challenged.

"Yes, I can," Penn said and motioned for her to follow him out the back doors into the yard. There was an old swing hanging from a live oak limb, and he motioned for her to join him as he sat in it. He tested it with a few bounces, and when he was satisfied that it wasn't going to fall, he held out his hand for hers.

She placed her hand in his and joined him. Her heart hammered in her chest, and her stomach felt a little queasy. Her palms were sweaty, so she wiped them on her pajama bottoms.

"I'm an angel," Penn said, and Livy's heart raced even harder.

"An angel? Like a heavenly angel? Are you from Heaven?" she asked in shock.

"Yes, I'm from Heaven, although I haven't been there in a very long time. My brethren and I were banished to Earth many eons ago. Have you heard of the Grigori Watchers?"

Livy shook her head. She'd been attacked by a demon only to be rescued by an angel. She didn't know whether to laugh or to cry. This was just too surreal.

"At the beginning, there were over two hundred of us, sent to help Adam and Eve after they'd been banished from the Garden of Eden. But, in time, many of our numbers fell in love with mortal women and men and took them as husbands and wives, starting families of their own—which was highly forbidden."

"Did you take a wife?" Livy asked and then berated herself. His personal life wasn't any of her business.

"No," Penn answered sadly. "I never found anyone I loved." Livy couldn't help but feel relieved at his words, and a part of her wished she was his mate. But she banished that thought from her mind. *Nope.*

"God grew displeased with us, so he punished us. He sent plagues, floods, warriors, whatever it took to kill off all Grigori mates and offspring. Many Grigori repented and returned to Heaven, but six of us remained on Earth to continue helping mankind, mainly with demon infestations."

"He killed women and children because the relationships were forbidden?" Livy asked, appalled that God would do such a thing. In all her church upbringing, she'd learned that God was a benevolent God, that He forgave and loved all His creations. What was a Grigori's child but a product of God Himself?

"It was forbidden," Penn repeated sadly. "A couple of my brethren still haven't recovered from losing their mates and children, but that's another story. Recently the apocalypse has been triggered, and the Four Horsemen are almost free. We can't have them escape Hell. That's why we need you."

"What am I supposed to do?" Livy's voice rose a couple of octaves, and she surged to her feet. "I'm a nobody. I have no powers. I'm just an ordinary person. How am I supposed to help?" She ran her fingers through her short tresses. She felt panic, that old familiar enemy, rising in her throat, and her heartbeat elevated to the point she almost hyperventilated.

Penn rose from his seat and guided her to sit down again. He retook his seat and rubbed circles on her back with his open palm. Although the action soothed her, her breath came in short bursts. She wasn't some great hero like in the books she read. She was just a plain, old girl trying to make it after losing everything dear to her. She shook her head. This wasn't happening. This *couldn't* happen. Thanks to reading paranormal fantasy all these years, she could accept the fact that she sat with an angel, and by accepting that angels exist, she could accept that she'd been attacked by a demon, but for the weight of the world to lie at her feet, that was too far.

"I can't," she whispered, her breath in small pants. "I can't save anybody. I couldn't even save myself."

"That's where you're wrong." Penn reached out and placed his fingers under her chin, directing her to look up at him. "You have all the power. You control the greatest army ever built. Just with a touch of your hand, you can guide them. Please say you're willing to try. Without you, our cause is lost. You're the last of a great bloodline that has protected this army for eons."

Livy struggled with getting her breathing under control, and along with that, the shaking in her hands and feet subsided. Her curiosity had been piqued.

"What am I supposed to do?" she asked and took a deep breath, expelling it slowly, pushing all the negativity from her body. If she was the last of some great bloodline, then that meant her mother or father knew all of this. One of them had known it all and never told Livy. Fresh heartache tore through her. How could they keep such a secret from her? How could they leave Livy unprepared and frankly scared as hell?

"That's the hang-up. We must find two artifacts that, when combined with you, will create an ultimate weapon in freeing this army. Do you have any idea where your mother would have hidden such treasures?"

"No," Livy said, speed-processing her mother's betrayal. She'd deal with it another time. Right now, she had other things to focus on. "I have no idea. There are boxes everywhere around here. I guess we could look, although I have no idea what we're looking for." She rose from the swing and turned back to look at Penn. "Any idea what we're looking for?"

"According to my research, we're looking for an ancient journal and a signet ring. They belonged to King Solomon, but he was tricked into having relations with a demon, which is—" His voice trailed off, and his face turned red.

"Well, come on, out with it," Livy scolded him like a child. There wasn't much more that would surprise her at this point.

"The Daughters of Lilith descend from King Solomon. The demon Lilith tricked Solomon into having an affair with her. That's where your bloodline comes from." He rose from the swing and shuffled his feet.

"Well," Livy huffed. "I'm descended from a demon. That just takes the cake." With that, she turned and headed toward the back door. "I'm going to get dressed. You can start with the boxes in the living room." She left him standing in the backyard, not sure what else she could do.

She stomped up the stairs and slammed her bedroom door, keenly aware that she was acting like a spoiled teenager. Well, wasn't that what she was? No, she was a spoiled demoness. That's what she was. How could she be a demon? She didn't feel like a demon. She didn't want to eat small children or drown old ladies. She felt like herself, in all aspects but one. She examined her feelings for Penn. She'd never felt like this before, so she had nothing to compare it to. What if it was the demon in her wanting to seduce the angel in him?

She'd been in Sunday school enough to remember the teachings, and one of the big ones—demons tempted angels to fall. So, were her feelings true, or were they a manifestation of something deeper, darker, and slightly evil? There was no way to know unless she pursued them. The mere thought of having a relationship with Penn set her blood on fire. Lava coursed through her veins.

Could she come to love him? Should she love him? Those were questions she desperately wanted answers to. She wanted him for sure. Who wouldn't with a body like his?

She dressed in jeans and a T-shirt, her favorite attire, and headed to the bathroom to look at herself in the mirror. As mornings of a short night's rest went, she didn't look that bad. She combed her hair, smeared on some lip gloss, and pressed her lips together to study her reflection. Was she pretty? Was she capable of seducing a man? She'd never done anything like what she was thinking in all her life. Not even as a younger teenager. Hell, she'd never been kissed a lot. She'd rather keep her nose in books and live in the different worlds of elves, dwarves, faeries, vampires, and werewolves.

She'd lived in her dream worlds all her life, and now was the time to live in the real world. With one last look in the mirror, she headed downstairs to help look for a book and ring that would help her save the world from the apocalypse.

****

While Livy got ready upstairs, Penn dug through boxes, but his mind wasn't on his task. It was on the beautiful woman just out of reach. He wanted her more than he'd wanted anything in his life—his very long life. She was the answer the world needed, but she was the woman *he* needed. He'd kept his hands to himself long enough. It was time to make a move. His mind told him to hold off, but his body and heart said to claim her. Although they had this monumental task ahead of them, he *would* make her his.

"Hi," she said as she descended the stairs. Penn looked up and almost lost his breath. She was so pretty. She wore her hair in a simple style, and far as he could tell, she wore no makeup, but she was still the most beautiful thing he'd ever laid eyes on. Without thought, without care of what others might say, he stood and walked toward her. He took her face in his hands and very gently laid his lips against hers.

He was surprised when her arms went around his waist and even more surprised when *she* deepened the kiss. Her tongue probed his mouth, and the sensation went straight to his groin. He hardened like a rock. He shifted his arms to hold her around her shoulders and pulled her even closer to him, letting her know just how much she affected him.

"Livy, I can't pretend anymore. I want you," Penn whispered against her lips. "It's wrong of me. It certainly isn't the time, but I can't think rationally when I'm around you."

She looked up at him, her bright green eyes innocent in so many ways, and then she smiled, a radiant smile that made his already thundering heart skip a beat.

"What took you so long?" she asked, her voice barely above a whisper.

Their lips crashed together in a tornado of desire. Penn tried to be gentle with her, but he couldn't control himself. His hands were everywhere all at once. He finally reached down and cupped her ass, pulling her lower body against his. She pushed him backward, and he landed on the sofa. She moved to straddle him, her hands in his hair, pulling his head upward to meet her lips again. He wound his arms around her waist and pulled her closer to him. He got lost in her kiss and only surfaced when she pressed her core harder against him.

He didn't want to take her on the sofa, not for their first time. He wanted to romance her, treat her tenderly like a lover should.

"Wait." He stopped her with a finger to her lips. "I want to do this right. I want to give you something romantic. Not a romp on the sofa."

She smiled. "Honestly, I don't need something sweet and romantic, I need *you*—now," she said and reached down to caress him through his jeans. He groaned low in his throat and laid his head back against the soft, plush cushion. He had no more control left in him. He wanted to surrender himself to her, and she was right—it didn't matter where or when. He grabbed her around the waist and quickly switched their positions, his body pressing hers into the sofa. She wrapped her legs around his waist and ran her hands down the length of his back to his ass, pulling him against her.

A low growl escaped his lips, and he leaned down to press another kiss to her lips. Among the swirling chaos of lips, hands, and bodies, a small detail popped into his head. He pulled away from her as if she'd burned him.

"We can't do this," he panted. "I can't make love to you. You're only twenty years old. I'm ancient. It would be like taking advantage of you, and that's not something I would ever do."

She sat up, her face flushed from their making out.

"Why does my age matter?" she asked with the sweetest frown on her face. "I'm old enough to know what I want, and I want you. Please don't make me wait." She reached up and grabbed a fistful of his shirt and pulled him back down to her. She pressed her lips to his throat and laved at the skin there.

Not able to withstand much more, Penn scooped her up and headed toward the stairs. They entered her bedroom, and he laid her on the bed. Standing back, he just looked at her—from her wide green eyes to the tips of her perfect toes. It was crazy. They'd just met. How could he want her so much? How could he think that taking her was a good idea? They were moving too fast, so fast that he couldn't apply the brakes should he want to. He was too far gone right now. His body craved hers, and that's all there was to it.

He was going to dive into those deep green pools and live there for a while. However long she'd let him. But he made himself a promise that when it was time to move on, he'd do it with gratitude for the time they'd spent together. He'd do it without protest, and he'd do it so that she maintained her dignity.

Chapter 7

"Have you done this before?" Penn asked, and her cheeks flooded with heat. She wanted to tell him yes, that she knew how to send him through the roof with arousal, but she couldn't. This would be her first time.

"No, I haven't," she almost whispered. "You'll be my first." All the reasons that sex was a bad idea flew out the window when Penn stood up and pulled his shirt over his head. He was nothing but muscles, all smooth skin, and abs that went on for days. Her eyes roamed over his large biceps and wide shoulders. He looked like he worked out daily, but she imagined his prowess came naturally.

Her heart hammered in her chest. This was going to happen. She'd wanted this since the first time she'd seen him. She just didn't know how badly until now.

She grabbed the hem of her shirt and ripped it off as quickly as she could. Penn's eyes widened, and then he fell on her with the brightest smile. They rolled together, a tangle of arms, legs, lips, and hands.

Livy moaned low in her throat as Penn's tongue found her navel. He lapped at it, the sight so erotic that heat pooled in the pit of her stomach. He ran his tongue inside to taste her belly button. Liquid gathered in the spot between her legs, and she scissored them to ease the building tension. Suddenly her jeans were too constricting, too much material between what she needed and the solution that would make her soar.

"Pants. Off," she moaned. "Help me take them off." Her fingers fumbled with the button.

Penn reached down and worked the button for her, then he leaned back and shimmied them down her legs and off her feet. He tossed them aside, and her underwear went next. His fingers played hell at the tiny hooks on her bra. She giggled and reached back to snap them apart with a single twist of her fingers.

"I'm all yours," she murmured and reached up to run her fingers through his floppy blond hair. He smelled wonderful, like a pine forest after the rain. He ran his hands over her shoulders, massaging them as he went. She wiggled underneath his weight as he pressed his body to hers. The single bed creaked beneath them, but Livy paid it no mind. Her thoughts were on the sexy man atop her.

Her roaming hands moved from his neck to his back, lightly scraping his skin with her fingernails as she explored the planes and contours of his taut muscles. His body seemed to vibrate under her touch, and she smothered a satisfied smile.

His hands found her breasts, cupping and kneading the small mounds. Her womanly parts warmed and tingled. Again, she scissored her legs, her body seeking that sweet release.

"Easy, girl," Penn crooned and ran his fingers down to the sweet spot screaming for attention. She groaned, and her legs shivered. Her arms stretched above her head of their own volition. "I'll give you what you need," he said and separated her curly hairs to expose the moist button of flesh beneath. When his finger found her most intimate part and slid inside, she almost floated off the bed from pure pleasure.

Her breath came in short bursts, and she tried to push her lower body down onto the finger currently torturing her with so many exotic sensations. Her entire body thrummed with tension as a storm built in her core. The pleasure was almost too much to bear.

"Penn, please," she begged, without knowing *what* she begged for. She just knew that something mind-blowing waited almost within reach. Suddenly her whole body tensed, like a wire about to snap, and then the whirlwind of pleasure was upon her, carrying her upward to see the stars. Wave after wave of heated nirvana washed over her body, sending her higher and higher.

"Enjoy it, love. Let yourself go," Penn murmured and pressed his lips to hers, his fingers continuing to torment her into a slow, sweet death. "You're almost ready for me." He suckled her tongue into his mouth, and she swirled hers around his in an exotic dance. When he slid in a second finger and then a third finger, filling her sensitive flesh and coaxing her already tensed muscles, her legs began to jerk and spasm. A fine sheen of sweat coated her body, and she trembled so badly she thought she'd shatter any second.

He pulled his lips from hers and whispered, "Almost there." Then he withdrew his fingers, and Livy almost screamed from the injustice of his absence. But before she could protest, his mouth filled the space his fingers had just vacated. He took her plump bud of flesh into his mouth and rapidly flicked his tongue over and over and over. Her pelvis jerked and quaked, almost like her body tried to keep a rhythm with him.

She reached down and grabbed two fistfuls of hair,

tugging on him. "Penn, I need...I need...Oh God, I don't know what I need."

He pulled his head back, and she gasped as cool air rushed over her overheated flesh.

"I know what you need, sweetheart," he whispered, his mouth blowing heated air on her ear. He gently took her earlobe in his mouth and nibbled it as he lowered himself between her legs. He nudged her knees apart and pulled them up on either side of him, her feet hooking together behind his back.

She dug in and lifted her lower body toward him, offering him easier access to her.

"Slow down, honey." Penn chuckled. "I don't want to hurt you."

Penn could've said her hair was on fire, and she could've cared less. All she wanted was another flood of pleasure, the feeling of him pushing himself inside her, becoming one with her. She wanted his body to blanket hers with warmth so addictive she'd never want them to separate again. She looked up into his bright blue eyes and silently willed him to hurry, but he only smiled, showing those dimples she'd come to love so much. She felt his hand fumble for his stiff cock. He slid his fingers back inside her, withdrew them, and then spread the wetness over himself. It was the hottest thing she'd ever seen. Her toes curled, and her legs trembled.

"Here we go." He guided the tip of his cock into her. A burning sensation tore through her midsection, and she swallowed a gasp. He froze. "Relax. It will only hurt for a split second, then you'll feel all the pleasure in the world," he murmured into her ear.

She made herself relax, her hot sheath settling

around him as he gently pushed inside her, one inch at a time. She took him all the way in as he slowly pressed his pelvis to hers until he filled her. He withdrew just as slowly as he'd entered, then lunged again more forcefully. The friction between them rubbed just where she needed it. She loosened her arms from around his neck and dug her blunt nails into his back, urging him to speed up. She needed more, faster.

"Hold on." He continued to pound into her over and over, in and out, heat and the absence of. It was enough to drive her mad. She felt that glorious peak ahead of her and struggled to reach it. He pressed his mouth to hers again, their tongues mimicking the dance their lower bodies engaged in. She noted a different taste on his tongue and wondered if she was tasting herself on him.

Suddenly a wave of heat burst through her, and she lifted her ass, pulling each thrust into her harder and harder. Her body convulsed, and she screamed his name as one massive wave crashed through her.

****

Penn gritted his teeth when her body squeezed and then convulsed around his cock. She was so tight that it was almost painful for him to move in and out of her. But he pumped and thrust, each movement bringing him closer to heaven, close enough that he could reach out and touch the separate world. When she screamed his name, he sat back on his haunches, grabbed her by the hips, and pulled her up to sit astride him. He guided her hips until she rode him with his guidance.

He leaned back on his elbows and braced himself so she could ride as hard and furious as she wanted. She tilted her head back, and the bounce of her perky breasts was so sexy he nearly lost himself just watching them dance before him. He gritted his teeth and held off. He needed a little longer with her. Hell, who was he kidding? He needed a *lot longer* with her.

He wanted her first time to be something she'd never forget. He wanted to know he'd given her the best experience of her life, that no other man would ever compare. Not that he'd ever allow another man to touch her. She was his—now and forever. He'd find a way to give her immortality. If her bloodline wasn't already imbued with longevity, he'd find a way. Forever wasn't long enough for him. He'd claimed her and he'd never let her go.

With his hands splayed on her hips, he pulled her up far enough so he could lie on his back, and then guided her back down onto his cock. When she smiled and resumed her bouncing, he reached up and cupped her breasts, moaning at their plump fullness in his palms.

Her skin was velvety soft and tasted like peaches. He handled each breast just to feel that softness against his skin. Her nipples were hard, and he grabbed them between his thumbs and forefingers, rubbing them in rhythm with her rocking hips. When he felt her tightening again, he let her claw his chest, and then she was screaming his name again. She was so loud, he was sure the neighbors knew his name by now.

At last, she collapsed on his chest, panting. He wrapped his arms around her and quickly clambered over her, flipping her onto her back. She writhed and moaned, clearly wanting more, so he drove one last deep thrust into her, pulled out, and then flipped her onto her stomach. He grabbed her ass with both hands, raised her hips off the bed, and shoved back inside her warm wetness.

She spread her arms wide, clutched the sheet beneath them, and begged him for more. He gave her everything he had. He pumped as fast as he could and as hard as he could, trying his best to satiate her. It didn't take long before he emptied himself inside of her while she moaned his name. It was a moment he'd never forget.

****

Penn was the first to awaken. He had Livy wrapped up so tightly in his arms that it was a wonder she could breathe. He didn't want to let her go. She looked so peaceful lying there asleep. He needed to report in, but that could wait. He wanted to stay like this for a while longer. Livy stirred, and Penn went hard at feeling her skin on his. They could make love for days on end and it wouldn't be enough to sate him. He'd still want her.

He thought back to all the things that ran through his mind while they made love, and he cringed. Had he really thought he could keep her forever? He wasn't so sure. He wanted her body, yes, but could he— should he—come to love her? Maybe. Only time would tell. Being one with her had made him crazy at the thought of someone else being with her. So, maybe there was a chance, an inkling of an emotion blossoming in his heart. He definitely liked her, but love?

"Penn?" she murmured sleepily. "How long have you been awake?" She snuggled closer to him, and heat stirred in his loins. He'd have to get up soon, or he'd take her again. They had work to do. They had to avert the apocalypse, or making love would never happen again, and that was unacceptable for him. He had to have her again and again. He knew he'd never get enough of her.

"Not long," he said and pressed a kiss atop her head. "I hate to be a buzzkill, but we have things to do."

"I know, but this is so nice I could stay like this all day."

Forever brushed through Penn's mind. He could stay like this forever.

She pulled back and pressed her lips to his in a quick pop and then rolled away to get dressed. He let her go, although every molecule of his body wanted to pull her back and make them both forget the impending doom the world faced. They could ignite each other's bodies till kingdom come and worship each other until the very end. But he knew he couldn't think like that, not when mankind counted on them.

He rolled out of the small bed and quickly dressed. He glanced at her over his shoulder and smiled when he caught her looking at him. He felt her approach and stilled when she wrapped her arms around him from behind.

"That was the most wonderful experience of my life. I'm glad it was you who gave it to me," she murmured. "If you're not careful, I might fall in love with you." She pulled away and headed downstairs.

Penn stood still for a moment longer, his heart pounding in his chest. He'd never dreamed of finding his mate, the one he'd devote his entire existence to. In his heart, he knew it was wrong to take a human as his lifemate, but like many of his brethren, he couldn't help the feelings swirling inside of him. God gave him his heart. Why would it be wrong to follow it? The question was always something he'd wrestled with.

Now it had more bearing than ever before.

"Are you coming?" came a shout from downstairs. Just her voice was music to his ears. He knew deep down he'd give his life to have her as his own. But first, they had to avert the coming crisis.

He headed downstairs to find Livy going through boxes in the living room.

"I don't think it's here," she said and sat down on the couch with a huff. "There are boxes everywhere. This is going to take us all day." She stood back up and started toward the kitchen.

"Where are you going? There aren't any boxes in there," Penn said and reached out to grab her by the wrist. She turned toward him, and his heart stilled at the tears in her eyes. "What's wrong?"

She sniffled. "I'm wondering what Mom and Dad would think of all this apocalypse stuff. Would they believe it?"

Penn pulled her to him and wrapped his arms around her, holding her tight.

"You sure took it better than I expected, I didn't know your mom and dad, so I can't say what they would have thought, but I do know one thing for sure—your mom was a brave woman to have been a Keeper. Bearing that type of responsibility is not for the faint of heart."

"Then why didn't she tell me any of this?" Livy looked up at him.

****

Livy stared up at Penn, focusing on his gorgeous blue eyes. He made her feel understood and safe, and he was the only person she had to talk to about any of this. She hadn't made any friends yet, but she could probably call her BFF from Davis Springs and talk to her. Of course, she may not take the world's impending doom as well as Livy had. Nor would she believe that Livy had just slept with the sexiest angel she'd ever seen. Well, he was the only angel she'd ever seen, but she knew none compared to Penn.

She also knew that she had no future with him. He was immortal, for God's sake. Yes, he'd told her it was her choice as to whether she wanted to be with him or not, and he'd given her the impression that he wanted to be with her as well, but she imagined all men said that when sex was involved. She'd lost her virginity, for crying out loud. She hadn't even had time to process that. She didn't have *time* to process it. If everything went like it needed to, and she ended up saving the world, she'd have to sit down and ponder on how she truly felt about it.

Yes, it had been her choice. She'd wanted him beyond reason—she still wanted him beyond reason. She shook her head and smiled up at him.

"Let's fix some breakfast. It's hard to concentrate on an empty stomach." She grudgingly pulled away from him and went into the kitchen to cook some bacon and eggs—brain food.

After they'd eaten, Livy cleared the table and loaded the dishwasher. Truth be told, she was procrastinating. Suddenly, she had a thought. If she was meant to wield these artifacts, that meant she had a connection to them, so why couldn't she *feel* them? Did she even have that ability?

"Would I be able to feel the grimoire and ring if I was near them?" she asked and closed the dishwasher. She turned to face him, taken aback when she realized he'd been watching her.

Penn stood in the dining room doorway, leaning against the wall. He frowned and ran his fingers through his messy blond hair.

Damn, he's fine, Livy thought to herself. She banished the thought for later, much later—if ever again. She couldn't have the distraction, not if she needed to stop the apocalypse.

"I suppose it's possible," he answered, then seemed to zone out. She waited patiently in case he searched his eons-old memory bank. Her stomach lurched at thinking about just how old he was. Eons. That was a long time to be alive. The things he must have watched happen with the world and mankind. She would've given up on saving the world if she'd had to watch all the death and destruction of the wars the world had suffered.

Penn snapped out of whatever trance he'd been in. "Yes, with your mother gone, you should have a bond with the artifacts, which means you should feel them if you're near them."

"Well, that should shave off some time," Livy announced and started for the stairs. "I'll start in Mom and Dad's room."

Penn nodded and followed her upstairs. They went past her bedroom, and she stopped in front of a closed door. She reached for the knob, her stomach in knots over invading her parents' privacy. Even with them gone, it felt wrong for her to be in their room, much less digging around for something.

"Hey, you okay?" Penn asked and placed his hands on her shoulders, kneading them lightly.

"Yeah, I'm just preparing myself," she answered

and turned the knob. She pushed the door open and gasped when a familiar aroma hit her in the face. The air smelled of her mother's perfume, and the room looked the way Mom and Dad had left it the morning of their accident.

Livy hit her knees, and her chest heaved when tears burst forth. She bent her head, covered her face with her hands, and let the tears out. Thanks to Penn, she'd pushed all the pain away for a time, but being in their room right now, she couldn't control herself. All the emotions she'd felt at their funeral came rushing back, and then just as suddenly, the tears stopped, and she jerked her head up.

"Something happened the day of my parents' funeral. I went into the older part of the cemetery while the diggers were covering the graves up, and I was drawn—that's the only way I can explain it—to an angel statue. It was life-size and so mournful. I reached out to touch it and all hell broke loose. The sky turned red, and fireballs shot across it over my head. The smell of brimstone and char filled my nose. It was chaos."

Penn came around from behind her and sat on the floor.

"I know. I was there," he said and reached out to take her hand. "I was disguised as the old man. I brought you home when you passed out."

Livy gasped and then smiled. "Of course you were. Is there anything you can't do?"

Chapter 8

"I can't protect you from any of this, and that is really what I want to do. But that chaos you saw? That was the Four Horsemen exerting their power. They're free from Hell but are trapped in the Nether. They're trying to get free, and that's why we're worried," Penn explained and massaged the back of her hand. She looked lost, and he wanted so badly to take her away from all of this. He damned the force that made her responsible for her duties.

"I'm sorry I deceived you. It was the only way I could tell if you were the Keeper or not. Also, I didn't intend on falling for you. That's a side bonus." He reached up and plucked a tear from her cheek, rubbing the liquid between his fingers. He wanted to take her pain, her confusion, her frustration. He wanted to take it all away and lock her in a room where she'd be safe for the rest of time.

But he couldn't.

Honestly, Sem was going to kill him when he found out Penn had made love to her. Sem would say it was a distraction they didn't need right now, and he'd be right. But damn if she wasn't the most beautiful creature Penn had ever seen in his life. The size of her heart alone was enough to make anyone fall in love with her.

He froze at the thought of being in love. Up until

now, he'd been adamant about not loving any woman. But now? The possibility didn't make him sick to his stomach. Maybe it was possible for him to love without worrying about her ending up dead because of him. He lifted his eyes to hers and found her watching him expectantly. He'd gone off course with his thoughts. Time to get his head back in the game.

"It's not your fault or your friends' fault. This is all on destiny. I'll do my part, and I'll do my best—" she said and lowered her eyes to his lips, which gave him a rush. "But I can't promise that I'll save the world. This all sounds so impossible. How do we know that it'll work?"

Penn huffed and sat back, pulling her into his lap. "The best is all you can do. As for how we know that this plan will work. We don't. We only know that we need the angel army to push the horsemen back to Hell. It'll take every angel we can free—that *you* can free— to do that. So, tell me, do you feel anything from in here?" He wanted to get her out of her parents' room as quickly as he could. She needed to get *her* head back in the game, and sadly, that left no time for her to mourn. He'd make sure she grieved properly once all this was said and done. Until then, he'd protect her with all the power he possessed.

She shook her head and scrambled to get out of his lap.

"No, I don't feel any voodoo vibes or anything. I just feel sad. Do you suppose we should glance through the boxes just in case my powers of detection aren't working?" She walked over to the dresser and moved some of the jewelry around with her finger. He knew her mind was on her mother, but what could he do? He couldn't make her concentrate. Then a thought occurred to him. *He* couldn't make her get her mind in the game, but he knew someone who could. Sem could work enchantments, even persuade the mind to comprehend things it wouldn't normally think. But should he call on him?

He watched her walk around the room, touching things here and there, fresh tears flowing down her cheeks, and he decided.

Sem, I need you. I need you to cast an enchantment on Livy. She needs to concentrate on finding the grimoire and ring, but she can't stop thinking about her deceased parents.

Are you sure? came an immediate reply. *She may not understand why you deem that necessary, and being a woman who would temporarily lose control of her mind, she'll probably be pissed as hell when she comes to herself.*

Penn frowned. He would be risking what they had together by doing this, but really, what choice did he have? Sweat broke out in a fine line above his lip, and his heartbeat thundered in his chest. Was he willing to risk it? No. But did he have a choice? He glanced up at her again, the sadness all but oozing from her pores.

Do it, he told Sem and hoped they weren't his famous last words.

Within moments, the air around Penn grew thick and swirled over him like a rushing wind, and then Sem stood beside him.

The Watcher leader had colored his mohawk bright pink, and he looked scary with all the piercings adorning his eyebrows and ears, but deep down, Sem was as serious as it got. Especially when it came to his duties. He slapped Penn on the back, and Penn nearly toppled over. The man simply didn't understand his linebacker strength.

"I have to get back to Sara. Are you sure about this?" Sem asked again and pointed at Livy standing across the room. Sem had frozen her when he'd arrived. She didn't need another shock, not today, not now. She needed focus and clarity.

"Yes, even if she comes to hate me." And she would hate him, but what had he expected? Forever and ever? He couldn't help his feelings, but she was human, and he wouldn't be able to watch her age and die. He wouldn't do it. He lifted his eyes to Sem.

"The fate of every man, woman, and child on this planet is literally in her hands. The world needs her," he explained softly. His heart was breaking. He just hoped she learned to forgive him in time.

Sem walked across the bedroom and placed his index finger against Livy's forehead. He said a few words under his breath and then turned back to look at Penn.

"It's done, but it won't last long. She's more powerful than we ever imagined. Her mind will fight it," he explained and then was gone as quickly as he'd appeared.

Penn offered up a silent prayer and approached her.

****

One minute Livy was consumed by grief, and the next, she experienced a clarity so pure she'd never felt anything like it. She was hyperaware of her surroundings and could just about tell Penn what was in every box in the house. A box in the attic drew her attention. Maybe that was what they looked for. She cast a smile at Penn and then brushed past him to head for the attic stairs. She hit the steps running.

The attic had been the selling point of the house for her dad. He needed a home office, and the open staircase at the back of the hall was a particular thing he'd liked. The spacious attic was another. It spanned across the entire house, and boxes sat haphazardly all over the room. His desk had been set up in the center of the room, and several bookshelves littered the walls. Lamps sat all over the place, but he'd needed more end tables to hold them.

She felt drawn to a stack of boxes just past the open doorway, and she started toward them when the house suddenly shook down to its foundation. Plaster and dust showered them from above.

Livy turned to look back at Penn.

"What was that?" she asked around the lump in her throat. Her heart thundered in her chest, and sweat broke out across her lower back. But her feet still carried her toward the boxes.

"What the *hell* was that?" It felt like an earthquake had split the ground beneath them. Another crash resounded, and the force knocked Livy to the floor. She jumped to her feet and closed the distance between her and the boxes.

"What is going on? Is it the Horsemen?" she asked but couldn't take her eyes off the cardboard boxes. It was like her attention couldn't be pulled away. Things were happening around her, dangerous things that she wanted to focus on, but she couldn't. Her mind wouldn't allow it.

"I'm going downstairs to check it out. Stay focused and find those artifacts. We need them now more than ever," Penn said and took off down the stairs. Livy grabbed the top box and lowered it to the floor. She didn't feel like what she needed was inside, so she slid it aside. Her fingers itched to look through it, but her focus was on something on the bottom at the far back. Another *BOOM!* rocked the house, and Livy had to grab for the wall to keep from falling again.

"Demons!" Penn shouted from downstairs. "Demons have surrounded the house. Livy, you need to hurry. I can't hold them off by myself," he added as he climbed the stairs. "Keep looking."

Livy began grabbing and tossing boxes, their contents vomiting across the floor in a rush of papers, pens, knick-knacks, and books. Finally, she reached the one she'd been digging for. She tore the top off and stared down at a smaller wooden box. She pulled it out and frowned at the symbol burned into the side. She'd seen it somewhere before but couldn't place it. It was a pair of angel wings with a sword through the middle, only the point of the sword was in the shape of a key.

She cast a glance at Penn who merely stared at the box in shock.

"You found it," he said. "You really found it."

A resounding *POP!* rent the air, and Livy's mind suddenly focused on the vibrating floor beneath them.

"What the hell is going on?" The clarity she'd felt was gone, replaced by a chaos of thoughts jumbling through her mind. She narrowed her eyes at Penn, wondering if he'd been responsible for her moments of focus. Had he put some angel voodoo on her? "Did you do something to me?"

"We'll talk later, I promise. Right now, we need to get to Bonaventure Cemetery. We need to free as many angels as we can!" He reached down and helped her to her feet, and she frowned at him. He'd done something to her. She knew it. She'd get to the bottom of it, just as soon as they completed their mission. She started to open the box, but Penn placed his hand atop hers.

"Are you ready for this?" he asked.

"Yes," Livy answered and opened the wooden lid. Nestled inside, she found an old grimoire, a signet ring wrapped in an oily cloth, and a list of the entire Keeper line back to King Solomon's eldest daughter—Basemath. She reached in and rubbed the old book with one finger, in awe at how soft it was.

"Sheepskin," Penn offered and took her by the arm. "Now let's go. The demons aren't the patient type, and they're coming through the veil as we speak." He pulled her to him and then motioned for her to head down the stairs. "I could fly, but people would see us, and we can't use the Nether because that's where the demons are. Can we go in your car?"

"Of course, we can. What an odd question to be asking at a time like this," she answered.

****

The garage door opened, and Penn stomped the gas. The front wheels of the car squealed as they peeled out. The car shot out and down the driveway and at least thirty little gargoyle-looking demons pelted them. Livy cringed at the sound of claws on metal and turned frightened eyes on Penn.

"They're going to get in before we make it to the cemetery!"

Penn gripped the steering wheel so hard that his knuckles turned white.

"Hold on!" he growled and steered the car under a

low-hanging tree branch. As he'd hoped, the demons weren't paying attention to their surroundings, so the branch caught the majority of them unawares and knocked them to the asphalt. The few that managed to evade the trap hovered in mid-air, their little leathery wings flapping furiously.

"Luckily, those weren't the demons we need to fear," Penn murmured and watched the rearview mirror in hopes that they didn't resume the chase. He put the pedal to the floor.

They arrived at the cemetery, screeching the car halfway into a parking space, and took off running through the new graves. They ran past Livy's parents', and she cast them a mournful glance. Then she and Penn ran through the gate she'd gone through after her parents' funeral. They passed rows of time-weathered stones and overgrown graves when suddenly Livy stopped short, and Penn nearly knocked her over when he collided with her back. He grabbed her around the waist to keep her from toppling to the ground.

She looked off into the distance. Penn looked in the same direction and saw Sara's stone angel standing in the distance. He could only imagine what she was thinking. But he decided she needed a nudge.

"Any idea where there are more angels?"

Shaking her head as if emerging from a dream, Livy looked straight ahead and nodded.

"There's more this way. There's a path we can follow." Then she took off at a light jog, and Penn followed.

They came to an area that was filled with angel statuary, and Livy stopped before the first one they reached.

She had the grimoire in hand and wore the signet ring on the middle finger of her right hand. She'd flipped through the spell book during the car ride, her mind deciphering the old text to English, but couldn't find anything on releasing stone angels from their prisons. She'd panicked and it had taken a great bit of patience to calm her down. Penn decided that all she needed to do was touch the angel, but the moment Livy laid her hand against the mossy, time-weathered stone, nothing happened.

Thunder rumbled across the sky, and Penn knew it wouldn't be long before demons crossed through the veil. With Hell's Gate unguarded by Cerberus, demons would be running amok unless Livy figured out how her magic worked. They were working on borrowed time.

"What can you remember about the first angel?" Penn asked as he approached Livy from behind.

"Well, my current anxiety wasn't an issue. I recall the sky filled with fireballs, a gale-force wind blowing me around, and I saw the cage in my mind. It was like I zoned out for a moment and stood outside the cage, watching the little bird inside. Right now, all I can think about is that the world is going to end any moment, and it's going to be my fault." She held the open book in her left arm and furiously turned the pages.

Penn peeked over her shoulder, and his eyes widened at the illustrations flying across the pages. King Solomon had controlled a nest of demons and he'd written many spells about them. Penn's fingers itched to get ahold of that book and read through it. He and Sem could learn so much from it.

But after. After all this was over. After the

apocalypse had been averted and the world was saved.

"There's nothing in the book?"

"I've read every page. There's nothing in it about how I'm supposed to receive my so-called powers." She turned to face Penn. "Are you sure I'm the one who's supposed to do this?"

Penn frowned. He'd done his research. He knew she was the one. He took her in his arms, his heart lurching at the close contact. It seemed like forever ago that they'd made love. He pressed a kiss to the top of her head and wished they could be back in her bed right this second. Damn Finn, the one who'd freed the Horsemen, and damn Cerberus for abandoning her post. He snapped his wandering mind back to the present and pushed Livy back to arm's length, his body objecting to the distance between them.

"You're the eldest daughter, of the eldest daughter, of the eldest daughter who'd last recorded her name on your list. It must be you unless you or your mother have an elder sister."

"No, we're both only children." She grasped the book tightly to her chest. "But I'd give anything to have an older sister right about now."

'I understand this is a little much, but you have to embrace it," Penn said and reached out to touch her shoulder. "That's the only chance we have."

She nodded her head and eased her tight hold on the book. She turned back to the statue and closed her eyes. After a few moments, she reached out and placed her hand on the stone, but nothing happened. She took a step away from the angel and studied it, her eyes narrowed thoughtfully. Then suddenly her face lit up with the most glorious smile.

"It's the ring." She gestured to the band on the angel's finger. "I touched the ring last time. That *must* be it. Maybe it serves as a padlock to the prison cell?"

Penn gestured for her to try out her new theory. Livy took several deep breaths and then reached out and touched the gray stone band.

The ground rolled beneath their feet, and Penn reached out to catch Livy before she fell back against him. A ring of heated air burst from the statue, spreading throughout the cemetery, blasting them in the face. Then a bright light burst free from the angel's head, shooting upward into the sky, turning the blue to red. The stone burst, the statue crumbling to the ground at their feet.

Livy stepped back, almost tripping over Penn.

"Did I do it?" she asked, her eyes cast skyward. "Why is the sky red?"

"What time is this?" came a voice from behind them. Penn whirled, sweeping Livy behind him. The angel stood with dark wings spread wide, a frown on his perfect face.

"Put your wings away," Penn said. "The year is 2016. A war is coming, and we need all the soldiers we can get. Would you fight with us?"

The angel smirked and gave a mock bow. "I sided with the fallen one. Are you on his side?"

"All the Grigori are Fallen, the Horsemen are free, but Lucifer is still stuck in the Underworld. We work to keep him there. We need every able body we can get. So, I will ask you again, will you fight with us?"

The angel shook his head and swept his eyes to Livy, where she peeked around Penn's side. "I side with Lucifer, but I thank you for freeing me, beautiful one. I am in your debt." With that, he disappeared.

"What just happened?" Livy asked. "Did we just free a bad angel?"

Penn shook his head and frowned in disgust. "Yes, apparently, he is going to be on the other side, but we can't dwell on that. You have many more to free."

Livy turned back to look at the crumbled statue, and her eyes widened at seeing it returned whole.

"How does that happen?" she asked.

"The statue was merely a prison housing the angel's soul. When you freed him, his essence escaped, and the stone returned to the angel's replica," Penn explained. "They will all do it, just like the first one you freed. We must get going, my sweet. You have a full job ahead of you."

Chapter 9

Three days later, and Livy had freed every stone angel in the world. Penn flew them to every cemetery that had stone angels, and frankly, she was more tired than impressed. They'd recruited a little more than seventy-five percent of the angels to fight on their side. The others had thanked Livy and then disappeared.

She'd asked Penn if they'd released enough to make a suitable army, and he'd merely shrugged his shoulders. Livy was exhausted and wanted nothing more than her bed. She wanted to sleep for three days straight, but she had a bone to pick with Penn. All during their trip, she felt like he was hiding something from her, something to do with her shift in focus. She'd asked him about it several times, but he'd merely changed the subject. Now was the time for answers.

Once they'd returned home, Livy had put the box containing the grimoire under her bed but kept the ring on her finger. She kind of loved the way it was designed. A black opal nestled into a simple, yet elegant twisting of silver that looked much like angel wings. It was the same symbol as the one on the front of the grimoire.

"Penn, we need to talk," Livy said and sat on the sofa. Penn nodded his head and sat in the wingback chair opposite her. "What did you do to me?"

"What do you mean?" Penn asked, his face the

epitome of innocence.

"You know what I mean, but for the sake of my sanity, I'll remind you. When we were looking for the grimoire and ring, I was in my parents' room, overwhelmed by grief. I couldn't concentrate on anything but the loss of them. Then suddenly, my mind cleared to nothing but finding what we needed. Did you cast a spell on me?"

Penn wiggled in his seat, a sure sign of guilt. "I didn't do anything to you, but I did ask a friend to help you," he explained. "Sem came and gave you clarity, pushing your grief back from your focus." He sat forward and splayed his hands. "It was the only way to hurry things along. I'm sorry it had to be done."

"It 'had to be done?' " Livy lurched from the sofa to tower over him. "Are you kidding me? You took away my choice, my free will. How could you do that to me? After what we shared, I thought I meant something to you—at least, I *hoped* I did." She crossed her arms over her chest to comfort herself. How could he do such a thing to her? All he'd had to do at the time was prompt her. She would've snapped out of it. She knew she would've.

"I want you to leave." She pointed at the door. "I need some time to think, and I don't want you around because you muddle my thoughts."

"Livy, I'm sorry. I felt it necessary at the time, and I only did it for your own good. Didn't you feel better?" Penn stood and closed the distance between them. "I do have feelings for you, very strong feelings, and I don't think it's a good idea to split up right now. You never know what's lurking about. I can't protect you unless I'm by your side," Penn pleaded. He still didn't get it.

He didn't get that what he'd done was wrong on so many levels. He felt like he'd done the wrong thing for the right reasons, and that didn't sit well with Livy.

"Please, just go," she said again and walked over to open the door. "I need to think."

Penn reluctantly walked toward the door, but before he went across the threshold, he took Livy's hand in his.

"Please be careful. You're not safe. I'll just be next door." He released her hand and walked down the steps and the sidewalk toward his house.

Livy slammed the door closed before she could see whether he looked back at her or not. She didn't need his puppy dog eyes working on her heartstrings. She was mad and hurt, and she had every right to be. How dare he! Just because he was a superior being didn't mean he could control her or her emotions. She should have known better than to get involved with him, and what feelings she had were now under question. Had he made her feel those too? Had he seduced her and then manipulated her into position?

She knew better than to love. She'd lost everyone she'd ever loved, and now Penn was gone as well. She cursed herself for letting him in, for beginning to care for him. She'd thought she'd meant something to him. God, she was an idiot.

Realizing she was madder at herself than at Penn, Livy decided it was time for a much-needed nap. But first, she would eat a much-needed snack. She went into the kitchen and grabbed a box of instant noodles from the pantry. Two minutes later, she was enjoying them while standing at the patio doors admiring the backyard.

Alone.

Maybe alone was how she was meant to live. Now that she knew God truly existed, she wanted to ask Him why He saw fit to take her parents? Why leave her alone and so afraid of loving and losing someone that she pushed the perfect man away from her? She almost choked on a noodle at the thought of Penn being the perfect man for her. Yes, she had feelings for him, but his lying to her was a big problem. She hated liars, and part of her decided that it was all for the best. That she needed to shove him out of her life and get back to normal, whatever normal was.

She yawned and decided that everything would be clearer after some sleep. They'd barely napped the past three days, and she was exhausted.

She tossed her garbage in the bin and headed upstairs for a quick shower before bed.

****

Penn paced his basement floor. He couldn't believe Livy had thrown him out, especially over something as trivial as a quick spell to allow her to concentrate. Surely, she was overreacting, but he was willing to give her some time to realize it. Being away from her was nerve-wracking, but in the end, it was for the best. He'd gotten too close to her, had gotten too involved with her.

Hell, he'd made love to her. Sem was going to kill him. Besides, he couldn't be in love, *wouldn't* be in love. It was a crime against humanity. It would be a crime against Livy. She'd be the only one in danger. Even after all the eons that had passed since the Great Flood, she'd be the one punished, and his conscience wouldn't allow him to harm a human, much less Livy.

Oh, he had to face it—he was bad for her, and he should probably just pack up and head back home. After all, he'd completed his assignment and was needed back in Ireland. Those guys couldn't turn a computer on without killing it.

He stopped pacing and took a seat in front of the big monitor. He slipped on his headset and hit up a video conference with Sem. After a few minutes, Sem's face filled the screen, and Penn almost laughed out loud. His mohawk was dyed like a rainbow, and he wore a fluffy pink boa around his neck.

"What the fuck you laughin' at?" Sem demanded, and his pierced eyebrows drew together.

"What are you wearing? And what did you do to your hair?" Penn asked.

"If you must know, Mr. Fashion Police, I'm spending time with my sister. She's never dyed her hair or been to a slumber party, so I am obliging her and some of the rescued angels. After being frozen and tortured for eons, they deserve a little R & R." Suddenly, Sem got entirely too close to the screen and scowled. "What's wrong with you?"

And it was like the man's gaze seared Penn's soul. He didn't know how to answer, so he fidgeted with his stress ball and squirmed in his seat. Here came the dangerous part. But, then again, Sem might take it easy on him since he was spending time with his beloved sister, and from the sound of feminine laughter in the background, Sem's party was having a good time.

"Livy kicked me out," Penn blurted.

"Why did she kick you out?" Sem sucked in a breath. "She found out that you had her spelled, didn't she? I told you that women don't like that shit. They'll have us by the short and curlies and want to believe that we'll toe the line. You fucked up but good, boy-o. I don't feel sorry for you one bit."

"That's part of it, but not all, but you have to promise you're not going to make a thing of it," Penn said. "Even though I don't understand what I did wrong, she still felt betrayed, and I'm not too comfortable with her being alone."

"Oh, my fucking Dad, you didn't," Sem shouted, spraying a bit of spit on his screen. "Tell me you did not. Penn, you never—*I* never have to worry about you crossing that line, so please, please sweet baby jalapenos, tell me you did not sleep with her."

"I can't tell you that," Penn murmured and continued pumping his stress ball. He could practically feel Sem's rage. "I think I'm quite taken with her. I mean, I think I love her, Sem," he admitted. "I'm so afraid she'll be taken from me that I've decided to come back home and leave her be. The army is free. We don't need her anymore, so she can go on with her life."

"You're a fucking idiot," Sem accused softly. "If you love her, and I mean really love her, then there is nothing more sacred than having her as your mate. You can't throw that away. I mean, don't get me wrong, I'm pissed as fuck at you, but I understand. I've been there. You can't run away from this, from her." Sem sat back in his chair, bringing his monitor closer to him. "She's already in danger. She's the Keeper, for crying out loud. Are you ready for your next mission?"

"Don't tell me," Penn grumbled. "You want me to keep an eye on her."

"Hell no," Sem scoffed. "I want your ass to bring her back here. We need her on our side. Not to mention that I'd like to get a look at that grimoire. Now stop wasting time and get!" With that, he disconnected the call.

"Well, butter my butt and call me a biscuit." Penn repeated a southern saying he'd heard on television. He had no idea how he was going to pull this off. He couldn't just storm over there and demand she pack up her belongings, that they were moving to Ireland. She'd probably kick him in the bollocks. No, he'd give her tonight to rest and think. That's what she'd asked for. Then tomorrow, he'd go over and grovel. Maybe she could explain why she got so angry and why what he'd done was so wrong. Perhaps if she realized he honestly didn't know, she'd forgive him.

Tomorrow everything would change.

****

Livy toweled off and put on her comfy pajama pants and tank top. She felt better being clean of all the drama of the past few days. She felt lonely, but it was her own fault. She'd sent Penn away. Could it be that he didn't understand why bespelling her was wrong? He was an angel. Maybe he didn't know as much about mankind as she thought. Maybe she owed him an explanation.

She huffed. She was tired of all the maybes running through her mind. She was tired of Penn, tired of men, tired of angels. She just wanted to sleep. But guilt reared its ugly head. She reached over and grabbed her phone, setting the alarm for eight the following morning. That would give her plenty of rest. Then to appease her conscience, she sent a quick text to Penn.

—*We need to talk. Can you come over about nine in the morning?*—

The response came almost immediately. He must have been on his phone.

—Yes, we do need to talk. I'll be there.—

She tossed her phone on the side table and pulled the comforter up to her nose. She inhaled the aroma of lavender and closed her eyes before the tears could form. The scent was fading, and she knew she'd have to wash and dry it again to put the smell back. That meant doing laundry, which was something she hated doing. But she was alone now, and everything was up to her. Responsibilities she'd never dreamed of were now hers.

Soul-weary, she sighed and rolled onto her stomach. She wished she could go to sleep and wake up to everything being different. She wished her parents were still alive. She wished she and Penn weren't on the outs. She wished the apocalypse wasn't pending, and she wished she wasn't the great hero Penn made her out to be.

She wished he was with her right now, but she'd been the one to send him away, so it was her own fault she was alone right now. She could be snuggled up to his muscular body right now, but no, she'd gotten pissy and sent him home. She felt a deep connection with him, but was it love? She didn't know. Couldn't it *be* love? Again, she didn't know. She'd sworn off love. Couldn't they just have a physical attraction? Deep down, she knew the answer was "no." She still wanted a family of her own, even though it meant putting her heart on her sleeve. She couldn't go through life completely alone—not loving anybody. It wasn't possible, and she'd been a fool to think otherwise. She made up her mind that she'd tell Penn in the morning. After giving him the chance to explain himself and her the chance to try and explain why it had been wrong, she'd tell him how she felt. She only hoped that he felt the same way.

With one last sigh, she shut her mind down and surrendered to the bliss that was sleep.

****

Livy awoke with her heart hammering in her chest and a fine sheen of sweat covering her entire body. She glanced at the clock, which said it was only two-thirty in the morning. She hadn't been asleep long. She turned her lamp on and looked all around her room, searching for whatever had woken her up. Then something grabbed her by her leg and dragged her from the bed onto the floor. She landed with a resounding *THUD!* Her breath whooshed from her lungs, and she gasped like a fish out of water.

She kicked with both legs and swung her arms, lashing out in every direction, but nothing was there. She reached down to pry her leg free, and her hand was knocked away by an unseen force. Confused as to what was going on, she tried to get to the bedside table, to her phone. But whatever had her wouldn't budge. Suddenly something hard hit her in the back of the head, and she almost lost consciousness. The knock was hard enough to render her loopy, and she stopped fighting, her body going limp.

A loud *POP!* resounded, and then she was being dragged toward her closet. She didn't have the energy to struggle. *Where am I being taken? Who is taking me there?*

"Please," she begged, tears streaming down her cheeks. "Please let me go. Who's there? Who are you? Why can't I see you?"

But nobody answered her. The force lugging her stopped, and suddenly the scene in her closet split down the middle. It was like someone had ripped a photo of the inside of her closet in half. Then she was being pulled through the split. Her bedroom scenery changed to that of an empty desert. The heat blasted her square in the face, instantly evaporating the tears flooding her eyes. Her chest squeezed causing her breath to come in shallow bursts as she was dragged across an invisible threshold. Once through, she gasped heavily.

"No!" she screamed, coming to herself and regaining her strength. "No, let me go!" She started struggling again. The unseen force had absconded with her quickly and without much of a fight. It had hit Livy hard enough to render her useless, and she was disgusted with herself for not fighting any harder. Well, she would fight now.

Suddenly, the force released her. Livy wasted no time rising to her feet, and she turned to run in the flash of a second, but she slammed into an invisible wall that knocked her back on her ass.

"Ah, He will be pleased," came a male voice from behind her. She glanced over her shoulder and almost screamed again. She shook from head to toe.

Her eyes roamed over the creature that stood behind her, his torso that of a human, but the head of a bull, complete with long, black horns protruding from his forehead. His legs were that of a horse or cow, and they ended in hooves. Smoke tendrils wafted from his flared nostrils, and red beady eyes stared down at her.

"Oh my God," Livy murmured and scrambled to her feet, facing the monster.

"Not even close," the creature said and laughed.

"You can call me Beleth. I control over eighty-five legions of demons. You can thank the shadow demon who delivered you if you can find him." With that, he let out a high-pitched laugh that filled the air and hurt Livy's ears.

Livy turned and tried to run, but her legs wouldn't carry her. She was too afraid. She wished Penn had stayed with her. She wished she hadn't made him go home. God, she wished her life was normal instead of this.

"Where are you taking me?" she asked the bull creature. "What do you want with me?"

"I'm taking you to our master. He is the one who wants you. Now, no more questions." He reached out and took her by the arm, his grip firm and unyielding, and dragged her through the rough terrain.

Livy studied her surroundings just in case she managed to get free. The sky was a sickly gray color, giving everything around them a depressing appearance. Rocks and scraggly grass were sporadically spread amongst the harsh dirt. Her feet were going to be raw by the time they made it to wherever they were going.

There were no trees. It looked like she'd entered a post-war zone. She was on her own, and she needed to get her act together.

Chapter 10

Penn jerked awake and looked over at his clock. It read three a.m., the devil's hour. His sixth sense told him that something had happened, but he couldn't quite put his finger on what.

Update, please. He mentally called through the Grigori party line. Many groans and curses came through until, finally, Sem quieted everyone.

There's nothing new to report, Penn. What's happening on your end?

I don't know. I just awoke out of a dead sleep knowing something was wrong.

Well then, check on your girl and then go back to sleep. That's an order.

"So much for him being a big help," Penn muttered out loud. He threw the covers from his body and rose to get dressed knowing there'd be no more sleeping for him tonight. He grabbed his phone off the dresser and dialed Livy. She didn't answer, and his heart hammered in his chest. Had something happened to her? He wasn't going to wait around and find out.

He rushed from his house and headed next door. Thankful they hadn't replaced the glass pane he'd busted next to the door, he slipped his arm through and unlocked her door. He pushed the door open and eased inside, wary of a flying frying pan. It was pitch black downstairs, so he felt his way to the stairwell.

"Livy?" he called up the stairs. "You didn't answer your phone, so I came over to check on you. Are you all right?" No answer came, and his heart lumped into his throat. He took the stairs two and three at a time until he stood before her bedroom door. It was wide open, and he saw that her bed was empty.

"Livy?" he called again and walked into her room. Penn looked at her lamp and saw that the power was still off. Her bedcovers were dragged from the bed with half of them on the floor. He checked the bathroom and then stood in the middle of her room at a loss for words or action.

She was gone. Something had happened to her, and he wasn't there. He didn't protect her like he'd vowed to do. Was he too late? There had to be a trail. He just needed to focus on the clues. He turned in a circle, taking in the room at large, and a sparkle from the closet had his stomach clenching in rage and fear.

Something or someone had dragged her into the Nether, and there was no way he could follow alone. He needed help.

She's been dragged into the Nether, my guess, by a demon. I need a team to go after her.

Sem responded immediately, *Hawk is training the twins, Zel and Zeke went with Luna to help Kurbane find Cerberus, and I'm stuck at the Compound. Gadreel is getting all the new arrivals settled. I guess I could send Barr and some of the arrivals who are ready to fight.*

I don't care who you send so long as they're ready to kick some demon ass. Penn's impatience showed. He'd go alone if he had to, against orders.

He loved her; he couldn't keep himself from loving

her. He'd get her back, and then he'd protect her at all costs. Nobody would ever harm a hair on her head. He just needed to find her.

Let me get everyone alerted and suited up, and then they'll meet you in the Nether. You need to suit up yourself. You don't know who or what you'll face. Be careful, Penn, we need you.

I'll be fine. It's Livy you should be worried about. She freed the angels. She could be forced to put them back.

I hadn't thought about that. Sem's voice deepened. *I'll make sure you have enough backup. Signing off.*

Penn rushed from Livy's house and back to his own. He went directly to the basement and across the floor, to the safe he'd had installed. He spun the dial and then ticked through his combination, opening the door to reveal his battle armor—a black body suit with built-in Kevlar, shoulder guards, arm vambraces, shin shields, and a black polycarbonate helmet. He always kept his sword with him.

He suited up and checked the time on his specialty watch. It showed barometric pressure, water depth, temperature, and the time. It could also connect to his main computer and be programmed to perform many more features.

Progress? Penn called.

Penn, this is Barr. We're still getting suited up. We had to go to the main vault to find more armor for the new arrivals. We'll be there soon. I promise.

I'll be waiting. Penn went over to the main computer and sat down, his armor squeaking in protest. His fingers flew across the keys, but it was all gibberish. He couldn't concentrate, not with Livy gone and in danger. His mind kept throwing situations at him, and they all involved her dying in his arms. He couldn't allow that to happen. He wouldn't survive if anything happened to her.

Sem was right—he needed to take a chance on love. It was his fault he was alone and had been alone all these years. He'd forbade himself to love. He was the reason he was alone, and he was the reason his love was in danger.

"What have I done?" he asked out loud, suddenly grateful nobody heard him. He couldn't bear to hear it from anyone else.

****

The demon lord dragged her to a spot where another split in scenery floated in mid-air. This time the edges shimmered like glitter under a bright light.

"No," she screamed and pulled back from his grasp. If he led her through another split, she'd never find her way home. She hadn't thought to leave Penn a trail to follow if he came after her. He might forget about her and just go home. He may think she left!

The creature pulled on her arm hard enough to dislocate it and stepped through the split. Livy closed her eyes as she was dragged through on his heels. This time the air smelled of fire and brimstone, and smoke floated everywhere. She heard wails and screams, and pleas for mercy.

They followed a blackened sidewalk edged by molten lava.

"Where are we?" Livy asked but feared she already knew the answer. She dragged her heels, desperate to get back to the split that led back to the dystopian land.

"Your new home," he said and snickered. "We're

in Hell, my sweet, where you'll stay until He either tires of you or you die." He turned to look back at her, his nostrils flaring slightly. "I hope he asks me to kill you." He laughed and continued to drag her along behind him.

"Oh, don't be so mean to our new guest, Beleth, my pet. Livy is going to love it here." A new voice came from the distance, his words echoing through the rock walls. Beleth dragged Livy once, real hard, until she stood before him, facing the most beautiful man she'd ever seen. His long, straight black hair hung down his back. His face had the most gorgeous features: a straight roman nose led down to full lips and a strong chin. His eyes were what captivated her the most. Also black as night, but glittering like the stars, they pulled her in and kept her mesmerized.

"Look, she's already speechless," he simpered. "For Father's sake, let her go, Beleth. You're hurting her."

Livy jerked her arm from the demon's grip and rubbed the spot where he'd gripped her so tightly.

"Who are you?" Livy found her voice. "Why am I here?" The man was beautiful. He could drive any woman to distraction, but she loved Penn. The only problem was that she had to work hard to keep Penn on her mind. This devastatingly stunning man before her was working some sort of magic. "And stop whatever you're doing to my mind."

"Impressive." He inclined his head. "Not many people can withstand my glamor. Forgive my manners. My name is Lucifer, and I run this place." He gave a deep bow. "And if you haven't figured it out yet, you're in Hell, my darling."

Suddenly his eyes widened, and he looked past her to Beleth.

"Where's the book? You didn't grab the book?" Lucifer pushed Livy aside and got right up in Beleth's ugly face. "She's utterly useless without Solomon's grimoire! Now go find it!" He shoved Beleth back in the direction he'd dragged Livy from. "And don't come back without it," he shouted after the demon lord.

Then turning back to Livy, he offered his arm to her.

"Come, my dear, let's get you settled. We can talk later."

Livy kept her hand and arms to herself and merely stared at him. After a few awkward moments, Lucifer tilted his head back and laughed. He then gestured for her to follow him, and he led her deeper into the cavern-like atmosphere. They walked for what seemed like hours when he turned right and walked into a large, open cavern lit by thousands of slender white candles. A huge throne sat in the middle of the room, and Lucifer walked up the red-carpeted walkway to the raised dais the throne sat on. He spun around, his white robes following suit, and sat down with a flourish.

"Welcome to Hell, my darling little Keeper. I hope you like it here. I have many jobs I'd like to ask of you."

"I'm not doing anything for you," Livy said and crossed her arms over her chest. "I don't work for your side."

Lucifer sat forward, a hard glint in his formerly charming features. "You will work for me, or I will make sure you'll never work for anyone ever again."

Livy's blood began to boil. She'd lost her parents.

She'd been pulled into a world she didn't know existed, locked in by duties she was ignorant to, and now she had the King of Hell bossing her around. None of it sat well with her, and it was about time she put on her fighting gloves and shoved back a little, if not a lot. She knew they'd never find the book; she'd hidden it well. So now, it was up to her to fight the battle.

"You can't kill me. You obviously can't use the grimoire without me," she explained haughtily. "So, here's what we're going to do. You're going to let me go home, you're going to leave me alone, or I'm going to bind you to me for the rest of my life. Your throne in Hell will go to someone else, and you'll be stuck in a cage. Do we have an understanding?" There, she'd told him. She felt like a badass too. She wondered if this was how everyone who fought back felt.

A booming laugh brought her back to the demon king before her. He laughed so hard that tears ran down his face.

"You're a brave little one, I'll admit that, but around here, bravery is stupid," he explained and stopped laughing. He wiped the tears from his face and manifested a staff from empty air. "You *will* obey me. You don't have the knowledge or expertise to work any spells from that book or you'd already have done so. So, your little demonstration of power is just smoke and mirrors. You will come around to what I want, or you will rot in a cage of your own."

"Try me," Livy threatened. She was scared out of her wits but unwilling to back down. She knew for a fact that there were spells in the grimoire on controlling demons. She just needed to get her hands on them. Her only problem was getting out of here and back home.

"Guards!" Lucifer bellowed, and two female waifs entered his chamber, voices of the damned wailing in their wake. They each wore long, white dresses that were tattered beyond being decent, their flesh peeking out in places that disgusted Livy. Even though their flesh was in a state of decay, they still had their strength. Each one grabbed Livy by the arm, and Livy squirmed to get free.

"Take her to her quarters and see that she's fed and clothed. She's going to be with us for a while," Lucifer ordered. "On second thought, put her in the Queen's quarters. That'll be more suiting her station here." He turned and left Livy gaping in his wake. She had to get out of here but had no idea how. But apparently, she'd have plenty of time to come up with a plan.

****

Penn stood in Livy's room, waiting for Barr and their backup to let him know they were ready. He sat down on her bed and leaned over to sniff her pillow, closing his eyes as he inhaled her scent. He missed her even though it had only been hours since they had spent three consecutive days together. He knew in his heart of hearts that he could spend the rest of her days with her, and it would not be enough.

We should be ready soon, Penn.

Penn nodded but didn't respond. It was taking them entirely too long to get ready. But he knew they'd had to get in the main vault and pull old Watcher armor. He also knew that Barr wouldn't keep him waiting unless it was necessary. His fingers itched to rip demon flesh from bone. His sword screamed for demon blood. His head was in battle mode, so he didn't notice the loose floorboard near the closet until he'd paced over and tripped over it. He bent down and pulled the board up. There, nestled in a towel, was the grimoire. He exhaled a small breath as relief washed over him. *They may have Livy for the time being, but they don't have the grimoire.*

"I'll take that," came a deep voice from the split. Penn backed away with the book held tightly in his arms. The creature passed on through and stood before Penn. "My master is waiting for that. Give it to me, and I will not harm you."

Penn chuckled and dropped the grimoire on Livy's bed.

"Where's Livy?" he asked and patted the book. "Where did you take her?" Penn knew where she was, but he wanted confirmation before he ripped this demon limb from limb.

"She's in Hell with my master," the creature answered. "You can't save her. You can't even save yourself."

He lunged at Penn, catching him around the middle in a tackle that threw them both over the bed and onto the hardwood floor. Penn willed his sword forth and shoved away from the demon by thrusting both his feet into the demon's head. It only knocked him back a few inches, but it was enough for Penn to get his sword to the demon's throat.

But before he could do much more than push the blade into the bull's outer skin, he was flipped onto his stomach, and the sword was pinned beneath his chin. The creature placed a foot in the center of Penn's back and grabbed both ends of the blade. He pulled back with enough force to choke Penn. But when the creature pulled backward, he gave Penn enough room to regain his footing. A big mistake on the demon's part.

Penn pushed backward with his legs, throwing the demon off his balance and off Penn's back. Penn swung his sword, but the bull blocked it with his vambraces. Then out of nowhere, a double axe appeared in the creature's hand. He swung it at Penn's stomach, but Penn danced out of range at the last moment. But he wasn't fast enough to avoid the backswing that caught him in the back of the leg. The axe blade caught him in the meat of his calf, and he went down hard. He tried to get back up, but the demon was on him, throwing punches to every part of Penn's body. Remembering his training, Penn curled into a ball and protected his head.

Suddenly, he was picked up off the floor and then slammed back down, knocking the breath out of him. He swung his sword at the creature's hooves, hitting the hock hard enough to knock the demon away from him long enough to catch his breath. He lunged to his feet and hopped on his good leg while blood ran in rivulets down into his boot.

The demon advanced again and managed to hit Penn on top of the head, knocking him down again. His world spun, his thoughts of failing Livy. He couldn't take this demon, not with his leg wound. He looked up and saw the demon's hand coming down again and prayed Barr would be able to get to Livy, then his world went black.

****

Penn awoke to the familiar aroma of Hell. Aches and pains like he'd never had wracked his body. Then his memories came flooding back, and he recalled the short fight in which the bull demon had bested him. He squirmed roughly, but the demon didn't lessen his grip on the cuff of Penn's armor.

"We're almost there," the demon said and laughed. "I'll be rewarded for bringing you and the book." Penn's heart sank. He'd forgotten about the book. He'd left it lying on the bed, and now Livy was in even more danger. He wondered where Barr and the others were. Had she seen anything from the Nether? Maybe she was just biding her time before they attempted a rescue now that Penn was in trouble as well.

Lost among his thoughts, Penn was suddenly dumped onto a red carpet. He looked up and groaned. He lay at the foot of Lucifer's throne.

"Well, well, what do we have here?" Lucifer sat forward and looked down at him. "On your feet, Grigori. Don't you know you're supposed to kneel in front of the King, not lounge about like a woman with nothing better to do."

"Careful, Lucy. Maybe I was dragged here, but I'm glad to be here," Penn said and ambled to his feet. His left boot squished where blood leaked into it, but he managed to stand on both feet, hopefully giving the appearance of being in the mood to kick some ass. "I know for a fact that the Gates are overrun, and several Grigori are helping keep it closed. Do you really want to fuck with me?"

Lucifer shot from his throne and closed the distance between them, putting his face directly in Penn's.

"I smell blood. Tell me, are you bleeding?" Lucifer asked, and sneered. He then gave a loud whistle. "Why don't we let the Hellhounds tend to you? Do you think Kurbane has time to tend them while he's busy defending the Gates?"

Penn willed his sword forth and shoved Lucifer backward before advancing on him enough to press the tip of the blade into the demon king's throat.

"I'm not playing your games, Lucy. Where's Livy? I want her and the grimoire, and I want you to leave them both alone," Penn commanded and reached out to grab a fistful of Lucifer's robe.

Lucifer's black eyes narrowed angrily. He reached up and pried his robes free of Penn's grasp and then pushed the blade away from his throat. Penn thought he was ready to surrender. Instead, Lucifer motioned for the bull creature to come forward and then smiled.

"Take him," he ordered. "Put him in a cell. We'll deal with him later." Lucifer turned, tossing the ends of his robes theatrically, and reclaimed his seat on the throne.

Penn started toward Lucifer but was stopped short when the demon lord grabbed him up by the collar of his armor. Before Penn could spin to defend himself, everything went black.

Chapter 11

A knock at the ceiling-tall stone door had Livy leaping from the king-sized bed she'd been perched on. She'd just sat down from searching every square inch of the room, looking for either a weapon or a way out, but had found nothing.

She rushed past the dresser made completely of human skulls and bones and waited in the doorway of the receiving lounge to the left of the door.

"Yes," she called. It wasn't like she could open the door. It was locked from the other side.

A key rattled in the lock, and the door swung open to reveal two skeletal-looking women wearing what looked like they once were wedding dresses. The dresses were now nothing more than dingy gray rags hanging from the women's small frames.

"Our master wishes to see you," one of the women said through a mouth that was nothing more than wide-open teeth.

"Well, if the *master* summons me," Livy murmured and started out the door. The waifs stopped her by each taking one of her arms. She shivered at the feeling of those bony fingers wrapped around her biceps but focused on putting one foot in front of the other.

They led her down the hallway, past blood-red pools of liquid containing human remains. The mere sight of bones and flesh floating on the surface was enough to make Livy want to barf, but she kept her eyes on the flagstone walkway and her mind on other things.

Like Penn. She wondered where he was. Had he come over to her house and found her gone yet? She hoped he didn't do anything rash, like try and find her. It was too dangerous, and this was something she needed to do herself. She'd get out of here. She wouldn't stop until she was back home.

They finally reached Lucifer's throne room and Livy wasn't surprised to see him perched on the cushioned seat, but it was the woman who stood beside him that caught Livy's attention.

Her long blonde hair hung loosely across her shoulders, reaching to her waist, and her almond-shaped blue eyes twinkled in the cavern's bright light. A petite nose led down to plump lips that smiled sweetly at Livy.

She wore a long white robe, which looked to be fashioned of silk, with sequins lining the low V cut from her throat to her navel, revealing a peek of her cleavage. The robe reached the floor, hiding the woman's feet. A small shiny crown sat atop her head and upon closer inspection, Livy saw that it bore the same symbol she'd found both burned into the box holding the grimoire and the cover of the book itself.

"Ah, shall I formally introduce you?" Lucifer smiled and offered Livy his arm. Without taking her eyes from the woman's, Livy ignored Lucifer and closed the distance between them.

"You're Lilith, aren't you?"

"Indeed, I am, child. It is so nice to finally meet one of my descendants," Lilith said, and Livy thought that even the woman's voice sounded perfect. She reached both hands toward Livy, but Livy hesitated to take them.

"Why haven't you met any of the others? You had to have met your daughter," Livy said. Lilith's face changed from serene to scary in the manner of seconds. She bared her sharp fangs with a hiss. Her blue eyes faded to black, as did her blonde hair. Her white robe melted into a red, skin-tight leather body suit, and her blunt nails elongated into razor-sharp spikes.

Then, just as quickly as she morphed into a true demon, she faded back to that of a simple blonde beauty.

Livy took a few steps in retreat. She wasn't afraid to admit that she was scared spitless of Lilith at this point.

"Forgive me. I don't have many emotions, but my daughter is my greatest regret. She was taken from me at birth, and I never saw her again. She led a good life and, therefore, went to the big mansion in the sky when she passed from the world. She is a very touchy subject with me. All the others were beyond my reach as well." Lilith moved to sit on Lucifer's throne like she owned it. "I've begged Lucifer to kidnap one or two throughout the years, but he's never obliged me until now." She moved her gaze to Lucifer.

"I've told you all in good time, dear," Lucifer said and bowed. "And I'll leave you two alone so that you can catch up." He turned and sauntered from the cavern.

Livy turned from watching Lucifer to face Lilith once again. What did Lilith want with her?

Suddenly, one of the waifs walked past Livy

carrying the grimoire, and Livy's heart lurched. They'd found it. She chastised herself for not hiding it better.

The waif laid the book in Lilith's lap and then turned and left them alone. Lilith smiled and waved her hand, beckoning Livy to her.

"Now, we have work to do," she said, and Livy's heart sank.

****

Penn snapped awake and jumped to his feet, taking a defensive stance. He had to stoop to keep from hitting his head on the ceiling of the cage. He willed his sword to him and turned in every direction, ready for an attack that never came. He studied his surroundings, mildly threatened, when he realized he was in a four-foot by six-foot cell that consisted of bedrock. The door was made from prison bars, so he walked stooped to it and jiggled it hard. Of course, it was locked, but he couldn't be blamed for trying.

"Lucifer!" he yelled through the bars. "Let me out before this gets worse for you." When no response came, he moved to sit against the back wall and think.

Zeke, Zel, Luna, and Kurbane were already here, and even though they were defending the Gates, he stood a chance of getting out if he could contact them.

Sem, I have a situation and need help. He called and waited. Finally, after about five minutes, Sem responded.

What's wrong?

I lost a fight with a demon lord and got dragged to Hell, where I'm currently in a cell. I think Livy and the grimoire are down here as well. I need help getting out so I can find them before Lucifer does something stupid.

A few minutes of silence went by, and then Sem

replied, *I'm sorry, Penn, I can't reach any of the others. They've blocked me. They must be having trouble themselves. I'll try to reach Barr. She was supposed to be waiting for you in the Nether.*

I'll be here, Penn said and huffed. He was in the middle of a clusterfuck. Things couldn't get any worse. He waited for what seemed like an hour before Sem's voice brushed through his mind.

Barr is on her way in your direction. They hadn't left the Compound yet. Something about not finding armor for all the volunteers. The good news is you have plenty of backups. Just hang tight. They'll be there before you know it.

How will she know where to find me?

Sem's laughter played through Penn's mind and gave him the chills. Sem was easy-going—if grumpy— most of the time, but if anyone dared to mess with one of them, there'd be hell to pay, literally. But what could Sem do to punish Lucifer? The man was the King of Hell, for crying out loud.

Her instructions are clear. Find Lucy first, and after she's done with him, he'll be begging to lead her to you. Just hang in there, buddy.

Then he was gone, and Penn was alone again in his mind. He hated waiting. It was his worst quality. He had time to sit and think about what Lucifer was doing to Livy. Penn couldn't protect her as he'd promised, and that ate at him. He'd failed her when she'd needed him most. Not to mention that he'd pulled the grimoire from Livy's hiding spot, which allowed Lucifer to get his hands on it, to begin with.

Livy would hate him for that alone. She'd had it hidden in a pretty good spot, too.

125

"I'm an idiot," Penn whispered to himself. He'd planned on confessing his feelings to her when they had their talk that morning, but now he wondered if she'd reject him. Had he given her any reason to love him? No, he'd pushed and shoved at her to do her duty, live up to her destiny. He'd not taken the time to get to know the Livy underneath all that.

He decided that he had no other choice than to beg her forgiveness, even if he had to do it on his knees. He wanted her, and it had taken him a lot of soul-searching to realize that he could have her. But if protecting her went anything like now, he was screwed. They'd spend their lives either shut up in the Compound or on the run.

No. He refused to put her through that. She had a short life compared to him, and he intended to give her the best of the best. He'd pray every day if that's what it took. Yes. She was his, and he owed it to her to give her the best life imaginable.

He rose to his feet and paced to the bars. Gripping them tightly, he tried to push them apart, but nothing budged. He tried again—nothing. He was tired of waiting for a rescue attempt. He needed to get to Livy now!

Somewhere down the hall, wails of agony resounded, and he grimaced. Two waifs floated by, whispering amongst themselves. They looked like two skeletal ladies on their daily walk, arm-in-arm, heads together. It almost looked normal.

He needed to burn off some of the nervous energy he'd accumulated, so he dropped to his chest and started doing push-ups as fast as he could, packing as many as he could into a minute. Sixty wasn't a bad number for an angel, but not exactly something to brag about. Was he losing his touch? He decided that he'd sat behind a computer too much and was losing his edge. How else could a demon beat him in combat?

No, it wasn't a battle under normal circumstances. They'd been confined to Livy's small bedroom, but still, he should have been able to more than hold his own. Not get knocked out with little to no effort from a demon.

He pushed out more and more until he dropped face-first to the cobblestone floor exhausted and his arms feeling like jelly. He'd get in a nice workout if Barr didn't arrive soon.

****

Livy stood before Lilith and shook her head.

"I'm not doing anything for you or Lucifer," she said, her voice firm and final. She still couldn't believe what they wanted her to do. After all the time she and Penn spent setting the angels free, Lucifer and Lilith wanted her to put them back. To banish them back to a life of being frozen in stone. With nothing more than their thoughts and feelings to keep them company. She refused to do it. It was an existence she wouldn't wish on her worst enemy.

"My dear, you don't have a choice," Lilith said and laughed. "You *will* do it, or you will suffer not only Lucifer's wrath but mine as well." Lilith rose from Lucifer's throne and approached Livy. She reached out and took Livy's chin in her hand, tipping it back so they could look into each other's eyes. "Believe me, I'm on my best behavior right now. You wouldn't want to make me mad, now, would you?"

Livy reached up and shoved Lilith's hand away, narrowing her eyes as anger raged through her veins.

How dare they threaten her? She held the power to make them bow at her feet. She just needed to get her hands on the grimoire. Before she thought better of it, she reached out and took the book from Lilith. She moved around her to sit on Lucifer's throne. Tired of being afraid all the time, she decided it was time to take some action. She'd show them her power, whether they liked it or not.

"What are you doing?" Lilith asked and a smile formed on her lips. She thought she had Livy where she wanted her, but she had no idea what she'd done. Livy aimed to show her.

Livy opened the book and began turning pages. The spell she was looking for was near the back. She found the page and ran her finger over the inscription. It was in a language she shouldn't be able to comprehend, but somehow her mind formed the translation.

"*Demonio, te praecipio*, Demon, I command thee," Livy said the words out loud, and Lilith lunged toward Livy and the book, but stopped short as the words spread their power. Lilith immediately dropped to her knees and bowed her head demurely.

"Now, that's more like it," Livy said and smiled. "Now, we just need to figure out what to do with you and find someone to take me home."

Suddenly, a woman dressed in head-to-toe black leather ran into the cavern, followed by an army of the most gorgeous men Livy had ever seen. She looked back at the woman, realizing she was just as beautiful with her brown, pixie-cut hair styled in a low mohawk and khol-rimmed green eyes. She carried a short sword, which she held out before her.

"Who are you?" the woman demanded.

"I'm Livy, and that's Lilith." Livy nodded at Lilith, then snapped the book closed and stood. "I was just teaching my so-many-greats-grandmother a lesson in humility." She closed the distance and stood before the leather-clad warrior woman. "Who are you?"

"I'm Barr," the woman said. "We were dispatched to meet up with Penn and rescue you and your book, but ah—" Barr leaned around Livy to glare at Lilith, still kneeling on the floor. "It looks like you have things well under control."

Livy chuckled nervously, and her stomach rolled into a tight knot. Now that she knew who the woman was, she wondered about the men standing at her back.

"Who are they?" Livy asked and motioned to the group behind Barr.

Barr smiled. "They are the angels you set free; they are our army." She turned and surveyed the armor-clad, armed men at her back. "When they heard that you were in danger, they couldn't get here fast enough. So, you ready to go home?"

"Damn skippy, pardon the expression. I've been trying to figure out a way home ever since I got here. I was just about to make Lilith tell me how to travel the Nether." Livy turned back to Lilith. "What am I going to do with her now?"

Barr smiled mischievously. "I have an idea. Make her tell us where Penn is, and then you can do with her what you want."

"Penn's here?" Livy pulled the book from her chest and opened it back to the page she was on before.

"He was waiting for us to meet him in the Nether outside your house. The demons made a slit that would lead them straight to you and the grimoire." Barr

129

explained. "But we had some minor difficulties and were late. By the time we mobilized, Penn had been dragged down here and locked up. So, it became a two-person rescue mission."

Livy spared Lilith a disgusted look and then smiled up at Barr.

"Well then, let's get this show on the road." Once again, she ran her finger over the foreign words on the pages before her. "*Haz mi oferta*, do my bidding, and show us to Penn," she said.

Lilith's mouth tightened into a thin line, and she struggled to her feet. She moved like a marionette. It was obvious she moved against her will, so the incantation must have had a strong effect on her. She stood and slowly turned to face Livy.

"I will get you for this," she murmured and started walking toward the cavern doorway. "If you will follow me," she called over her shoulder, and Livy, Barr, and the angel army fell into step behind her.

****

Penn completed his nine-hundredth round of push-ups and sat back on his haunches. Sweat drenched his body, but he paid no mind to the discomfort. He suffered more mentally than he did physically. He'd tried contacting Sem, but nothing. He was beginning to think they'd forgotten about him when voices resounded from down the hallway.

He stood and rushed to the bars, putting his face as close to looking through as he could. He couldn't make out who or what was talking, so he backed up and willed his sword to his hand. He was prepared for anything but the beautiful face that ran to the bars and squealed.

"Penn! We found you. Are you all right? What have they done to you? You're all sweaty and dirty. Did they torture you?" Livy rattled off the questions so quickly that he couldn't keep up, so he went to the bars and grabbed her hands.

"Shh. I'm okay. I was just exercising to pass the time," he reassured Livy and then looked over her head and gasped when he saw Lilith, Barr, and an army of angels. "Well, it's about time," he said and smiled. "Can we get me out of here?"

Livy turned to face Lilith. "Open the door," she demanded in a stern voice. Penn had never heard her use that voice before. It was a sign that she'd found her inner strength. He watched and waited for Lilith to unlock his cell, but she merely stood her ground.

Lilith smiled wide enough to show fangs. "I can't. Only Lucifer has the keys, and he won't be so easy to tame." Then she threw her head back and laughed so loudly that the walls shook. Dirt rained down on them as her voice ricocheted around them.

"Well, fu—" Penn stopped mid-word and locked eyes with Barr. "Can you find him? I want Livy to stay here with me. I don't want her out of my sight again."

"Where is he?" Livy questioned Lilith. "Where would he be? I know you know, so tell me."

Lilith's smile faded. She probably hadn't thought about Livy asking more questions that she'd have to answer. Her mouth worked a few times like she was trying not to say anything, but in the end, Livy's spell must have been strong, because Lilith snarled.

"He's in the King's quarters," she spat and then smiled again. "He's also guarded by the strongest demons we have."

"Thank you." Barr patted Lilith on the head like the good dog she was. "We'll be prepared. I'll make sure and send Lucifer your regards, Lilith." Then she turned to the army at her back. "Half on me, the others stay here with Penn and Livy." She gave orders like she'd been born to lead, and Penn smiled, glad that she was back in action. For most of the past five years, she'd been in her hawk form and shadowed Luna as her eyes in the sky.

Now that Luna had come into her Archangel powers, she didn't need nor want any backup, and that had saddened Barr to the point that she'd stopped training and going on missions. She'd taken to staying in her quarters. As far as Penn knew, this was the first action she'd seen in a while. He exhaled the breath he'd been holding since being dragged to Hell. Maybe with the taste of battle still on her lips, she'd get back into the swing of things.

Two of the angels moved to flank Lilith, and the demoness sneered at them.

"You think two angels are enough to control me?" Lilith asked and moved closer to Livy. Livy didn't retreat. She stood her ground and grasped the book closer to her chest. "I will kill you for this, descendant or not. You don't deserve to have that book. How dare you use it on your kind." Lilith spat.

Livy placed her free hand on Lilith's chest and shoved her back.

"Careful, or I'll really humiliate you," she said, and Penn smiled at her back. His little, shy woman had indeed found her strength, and now she employed it against one of the meanest and deadliest demons Hell had to offer. He was so proud that he wanted to applaud, but he didn't want to break the scene. He wanted to see where Livy was taking the conversation.

"I'll make you bow and kiss my ass with all your little demon minions watching," Livy said. "Don't push me, and don't you dare threaten me, especially with me holding the one thing that can destroy you."

Lilith laughed again. "You think I haven't been under this spell before? Solomon used it against me when he took my child, and he used it when he banished me back to Hell. I've endured much worse than you can dish out, Little One. You're an amateur at best."

Lilith crossed her arms and merely stared at Livy, silently daring her to do her worst.

Livy turned to face Penn, her face red and her lips pressed into a tight line. She looked furious, and Penn was afraid of what she was about to do.

"Whatever it is, Livy, it's not worth it. *She's* not worth it. She's just trying to yank your chain because you have her by the short and curlies. You're in control, and she knows it—we *all* know it. Just take a deep breath."

Livy seemed to consider his argument, and his heartbeat returned to normal. He couldn't protect her right now, not from behind the bars, so he needed her to calm down before she did something more dangerous than pissing off a hellcat of a demon. They needed to get the hell out of Hell.

Livy turned to once again face Lilith.

"Penn, how many demons are here in Hell?" she asked, and Penn frowned. Where was she going with this?

"I would guess millions of millions. Why?"

Lilith threw her head back and laughed again. "You can't possibly be thinking what I think you're thinking, little girl. The Gatekeeper is missing, so there's a free-for-all at the Gates. Demons are rushing it in hordes."

Livy smiled and turned to look at Penn.

"Well then, we must help in any way we can, right?"

Chapter 12

Livy couldn't have thought of a better plan. This was the perfect way to show them all.

"I'm going to the Gates. Come find me when they let you out." Livy stood outside of Penn's reach. She knew he would try to stop her, and this was something she needed to do. Her blood pounded through her veins, magic imbuing every molecule of her body. She now understood why Solomon had not let the grimoire out of his sight. The power was seductive, but she was strong enough to withstand that. She'd help the Grigori in the only way she could.

"Take me to the Gates," Livy commanded Lilith. She turned to face Penn one more time and smiled.

"I'll be fine, promise."

"No!" Penn shouted. "No, Livy, don't do it! I can't protect you from in here! Come back," he yelled at the top of his lungs, but Livy merely blew him a kiss and fell into step behind Lilith. The angels that Barr had left behind all shared confused looks amongst themselves, obviously torn between following Livy and waiting with Penn. In the end, half the group broke off and fell into step behind Livy.

"See?" she called over her shoulder to Penn. "I'll be fine." She would never forget the rage on his face as he watched her walk away. She was going to have a hard time making it up to him, but he would get over it.

If she was going to be a part of his life, she was going to pull her weight. She refused to cower behind him any longer.

She held the book tightly to her chest and followed Lilith through the worst parts of Hell. There were pits where voices of the damned begged anyone to set them free. They swore they'd repent and were sorry for their actions, but the demons guarding them merely tossed rocks into the abyss and laughed.

Then there was the area where souls were being disemboweled. Blood and gore coated the walls and floors, and large vats containing body parts sloshed as more bits were thrown in. Livy caught herself gagging more than once and cursed Lilith as the demoness cast knowing smiles in her direction.

She was doing this on purpose. Livy had demanded to go to the Gates, but Lilith was taking the most gruesome route she could think of, and that was fine with Livy. She'd soldier through.

The next display was where heads were stored on pikes, while lifeless bodies sat below them. Their stomachs were sliced open, and their guts were strewn all over the place. Livy accidentally stepped on something slippery and nearly fell on her ass. If it hadn't been for the angel who caught her, she would have humiliated herself. She murmured a "thank you," and then rushed to catch up with Lilith who acted like she was on a stroll through the Queen's gardens.

"What's the matter, dear? See something that upsets you?" Lilith asked sweetly.

"There's nothing you can throw at me that I won't power through. Just remember that, Grandma," Livy tossed back and laughed when Lilith's back straightened.

They finally arrived at the Gates, and Livy's eyes widened at seeing the two creatures guarding it. One was a demon resembling the one who dragged her to Hell. He was a bull from the head up and waist down. The only human part about him was his torso. Livy blushed when she noticed his manly parts were bare and dangling in the open air.

The other creature was the scary one. He looked like a true badass. From the top of his raven hair falling down and over his shoulders, to the eyebrow rings and silver hoop in one nostril. He also had his lower lip pierced with a bar through it. The jewelry didn't distract from his otherwise perfect face—he looked like a Greek God. His eyes were red, rimmed in black, and narrowed in anger. He was well over six feet tall. Broad, muscular shoulders showed through his torn shirt, and his biceps had to be bigger than her thighs. He carried a double-headed axe, and the entire thing was covered in blood and gore. She wondered how long he'd been fighting back demons.

One of the vile creatures made a run for him, and with little effort, he swung the axe, beheading the thing in one swing. If she weren't in awe, she would have been terrified.

"Who the fuck are you?" he snarled and eyeballed another demon as it stood a good distance off, but ready to run.

"I'm Livy, the Keeper. I've come to help you with your demon problem," she said and slowly approached him. He glared at her, his eyes roaming from the top of her head to the bottom of her feet. He suddenly threw his head back and laughed.

"What are you going to do, sweetheart? Throw your book at them?"

"I'm going to bespell them, Mr.—?"

"Kurbane, the son of Cerberus," he offered with an eyebrow raised.

"Kurbane, I can control demons with the spells in this book. I'm going to make the Gates off-limits to them," Livy explained and nearly laughed at the bug-eyed look Kurbane gave her.

"You can do that?" he asked, and she nodded. "If you can, I would be very grateful. Instead of fighting these monstrosities, I could be looking for my mother." He swung at another demon who rushed him, but this one gave him a fight.

Kurbane swung the axe at the demon's neck and the demon danced out of reach. The demon then swung his sword at Kurbane, hitting him in the back and Kurbane grunted and fell to his knees. He stuck the end of the axe in the ground and used it as a crutch to regain his footing.

"I'd be much obliged if you'd start soon," he yelled and twirled to hit the demon in the stomach as it rushed him from behind.

Blood spattered Livy, drenching her shirt, her face and neck, and the front of her pants. She looked down at the book, and her eyes widened as the blood covering it soaked into the leather almost like the book drinking it. There was still so much she didn't know about the book and Solomon. She'd just chalk this incident up to learning on the run. Maybe the blood would make the spells more powerful. She'd never know if she didn't get her ass in gear.

She flipped the cover open, found the page she was

looking for, and began chanting.

****

Penn had never been so angry in all his life. Once Barr freed him from his cell, he started searching for the Gates. He was glad that his leg had had time to heal, but he didn't know the way and was utterly lost until he and Barr wrangled a demon and made it show them the way. If they'd just stayed on the path leading past Lucifer's throne room and Penn's cell, they would have found the Gates on their own. Going that route, it didn't take long to get there, and when Penn's eyes landed on Livy, his heart exploded in his chest.

She was covered in blood. Was it her blood? What had happened to her? Penn was going to kill somebody or something.

She stood near Kurbane, who was engaged in fighting off four demons at once. The demon helping Kurbane had his hands full with five of his own. It was a melee of blood, guts, and gore. Livy was oblivious to everything but the book. She didn't so much as look up the whole time she stood there.

Penn willed his sword and ran to her. He shoved her behind him and took up a defensive position. Barr and the rest of the angel soldiers formed a line across the Gates, each one raising their weapon.

Suddenly, the small demon hordes morphed into large demon hordes, and it seemed like all of Hell rushed the Gates at the same time. Penn hurried to meet a demon, swinging his sword with fluid expertise. He caught the demon across the throat, beheading him in his tracks. Then, just as quickly as one disappeared, two more took its place. All his fighting skills went out the window as he tried to do nothing more than keep the demons away from Livy while she did her thing. Whatever it was, he hoped that it worked, or else they'd all be dead.

He was mid-swing with a demon when a blast of inferno-like heat hit him square in the back, knocking him to the ground and the demon away from him. He looked around and saw that Kurbane and Amon, as well as Barr and the angels were also on the ground and that all the demons were gone.

He lunged to his feet and turned to find Livy. She still remained in the same place she'd been, and after a look around, Penn noticed she was the only one still standing. Lilith was also face-down on the blood-soaked ground.

"What happened?" Penn asked Livy. "What did you do?"

"I placed a spell of repulsion on the Gates. No demon can come near them now," she explained and smiled, obviously quite pleased with herself.

"Then why is she, Kurbane, and Amon still here?" Penn nodded at Lilith. "Shouldn't they be gone too?"

Livy looked around and frowned. "I suppose they aren't all full demon. I honestly don't know. All this is new to me."

"Then why did you cast the spell?" Penn demanded and closed the distance between them. "Why are you playing with this thing? It's dangerous!" He reached out, intending to take the book away from her, but she must have sensed his intentions because she snatched it close to her chest.

"Stop it," she yelled. "I don't need protecting, Penn. I'm capable of taking care of myself."

Penn's heart sank at her words. She didn't need

him to protect her, but that didn't mean he'd ever stop trying. Even if he had to fight her tooth and nail. Besides, they had other things to talk about.

"Fine," Penn said and backed up a step. "You may be capable of taking care of yourself, but that doesn't mean I won't cover your back. What do you say to being partners?" He offered his open hand. She stared at him for a long time, then finally nodded her head in agreement. She took his outstretched hand with hers and shook it.

"Can we go home now?" Barr asked as she approached them. "I don't know about you all, but I'm sick of Hell."

Penn turned back to Livy and raised his eyebrows. Livy gave him another nod.

"We're ready," Penn called over his shoulder. "But Livy and I have some things to discuss, so we'll be going back to my house."

"Why your house? What's wrong with mine?" Livy demanded and frowned. She opened her mouth, and Penn placed his finger against her lip to hush her before she started yelling at him again.

"Your house has a portal to the Nether. Have you forgotten that?" he asked and moved closer to her. Their bodies now touched, and it felt so good to be near her again. He lowered his face to hers and pressed a soft kiss to her lips. He sighed when she kissed him back. She might have been upset with him, but she would come around when he had the chance to tell her exactly how he felt about her.

"I still need to hide the book," Livy said and pulled it back far enough to look at it. Penn didn't miss the lust that filled her eyes. The power was seduction, and after using the book, she needed to put it away for a bit, or it would overwhelm her.

"Why don't you send it with me?" Barr asked and opened her hands. "I promise you there's no safer place than the vault at the Compound. It will be there whenever you need or want it."

At first, Livy grasped it tightly and started to say no, but Penn placed his hand on her shoulder and gave her a quick nod when she looked up at him.

"It will be safe there. I promise," he murmured.

****

Livy wasn't sure about letting the grimoire out of her sight. What if someone else tried to use it? Would it work for anyone else? A fierce possessiveness rose from the pit of her stomach when she thought about someone else using it, and she narrowed her eyes. It felt like the grimoire had taken root in her soul, and she couldn't bear to part with it.

"No, I think I'll keep it for now," Livy heard herself say. It was almost like she was outside of her body, looking in. Like another entity had taken over. She looked down at her arms, surprised when she saw tendrils of magic running through her skin to the grimoire. No, she couldn't see herself living without the book or the ring.

"Livy, you really should let Barr take the grimoire. I don't think it's healthy for you to keep it any longer than necessary. Should we find ourselves in a position where it's needed, you will find it in your hands without hesitation," Penn explained and reached out to take the book.

Livy looked up at him, frowning when she saw the concern in his eyes. He was worried about her. He wasn't trying to control her. Maybe that had been his problem all along. He cared, and he wanted to protect. Could that be it? Was she wrong about him? She knew she loved him and hadn't had the chance to tell him yet.

It was like clarity had finally set in, and she saw the grimoire for what it was. It was a stain on the soul of whoever used it. Yes, it had its uses, but no, she didn't want to hold onto it any longer than necessary. She didn't know Barr well enough to trust her, but Penn did, and Livy trusted him.

Against her better judgment, she forced her arms out for Barr to take it, her eyes silently pleading with the warrior to take care of it.

"Don't worry," Barr said. "I'll protect it with my life." Then she turned and headed off the way they came, with the angel army trailing in her wake.

"Should I get Lilith to lead us back to the throne room? I think I can find the slip into the Nether from there," Livy told Penn. He nodded once and held up a finger for her to wait. He then ran over to where Kurbane and the other demon talked amongst themselves. He shook hands with Kurbane and then clapped him on the back.

He came back wearing a jovial smile.

"Yes, you can have Lilith lead us back, but I think I can remember the way," Penn said and reached down to take Livy's hand in his.

"Lilith," Livy said and turned to face the demoness. "I don't know how you're still standing so close to the Gates, but I will need you to lead us back to the throne room."

"Long as you're ready to see all the gory details of life around here, again," Lilith said and smiled sweetly.

"I don't think you handled it so well the first time around."

"Gory details?" Penn echoed the demoness. "What 'details' is she talking about? We didn't see anything but cavern walls that wind on forever before they led here."

Livy's gaze whipped to Lilith. "I knew it!" she spat. "I knew you were torturing me. Lead us out the right way, immediately." Then she looked up at Penn. "I can't wait to get out of here, and I hope I never have to come down here again."

"Oh, you'll be back," Lilith promised. "So long as I draw breath, I will torture you."

"I think I have an idea," Penn said and smiled. "Let's go."

Lilith did as she was commanded and led them back the boring way, which was fine by Livy. She didn't think she would have been able to see all the blood, guts, gore, and brains again. Once they were back to Penn's cell, Livy shoved Lilith into it and smiled at her through the bars.

"You will stay here until I give you permission to leave, is that understood?"

"NO!" Lilith screamed at the top of her lungs and beat her fists against the bars. "You will not leave me like this! Stop the curse. Let me out. I won't bother you again! Please?"

They walked off toward the throne room, listening to her cries and pleas. Livy didn't know about Penn, but Lilith's pleas were music to her ears.

"I didn't get to tell you what Lilith and Lucifer wanted with me." Livy tried to make conversation, so she wasn't thinking about Lilith's other direction.

"They wanted me to reimprison all the angels. Can you believe that?" she asked and then shook her head.

"Yes, I can," Penn answered and shook his head in unison with hers. "I figured it was something like that. They didn't harm you, did they? It's not too late to go back and kick some ass." He stopped walking in his tracks and looked down at her. His tone was serious, and he waited on an answer.

"Oh no, they didn't hurt me, just scared me a little bit. I'll probably have nightmares for a while, but nothing I can't handle," she said and smiled up at him. "Can we please just go home?"

Penn smiled and brought their joined hands to his mouth where he kissed the back of hers.

"Yes, I suppose it's time we have that heart-to-heart you wanted," he said.

They continued walking together down the corridor until they came upon the throne room, which was empty, so they kept moving. Livy's heart hammered in her chest as she worried about running into more demons, but Penn acted like they were on a moonlit walk.

"I seem to remember you wanted to talk too," Livy said, and Penn chuckled.

"Yes, love, I wanted to talk as well."

They found the tear that led them to the Nether, and then the one that entered her bedroom closet. Once they were through, Penn advised that she pack enough so that she didn't have to come back for a while.

"What about the backyard? We didn't finish it," Livy said and walked over to her window to peer down at the potted plants and shrubs. "They'll die if I just leave them."

"Don't worry," Penn said as he walked up behind her. "We'll figure something out. We have to get that tear into the Nether taken care of as well. It can't stay there."

Livy nodded her head and set about packing a rather large duffel bag. She made sure she grabbed her phone and charger, toiletries, enough clothes for two weeks without washing, her parents' banking information, and her passport. She grabbed her purse on the way out the door, and they headed over to Penn's house.

He unlocked and opened the door, then motioned for Livy to wait on his porch. He eventually came back out, grabbed her bag, and told her to follow him. He led her inside, dropped her bag on a rather bland, blue sofa, and walked on straight. Livy dropped her purse beside the bag and followed him.

She came upon him standing in the kitchen, back facing the kitchen sink, while he devoured a can of soda.

"Vile things. I hate them," he said and tossed the empty can in the trash bin.

"Then why do you drink them?" Livy asked.

"The house came fully stocked, so instead of wasting time with complaining or grocery shopping, I merely accepted what was." He pushed off the sink and closed the distance between them, where he took her face in his hands. "We have so much to talk about, but it feels like I've been waiting so long to kiss you." With that, he pressed his lips to hers once, then he slanted his head and used his tongue to taste Livy's lips. Her body shuddered in pleasure, and she opened her mouth, allowing him all access to a whirlwind of sensations.

Livy pulled at his top, not sure how to remove his battle gear, but Penn just placed his hand over hers.

"Why don't I go change out of this, and we can talk, okay?" he asked, and she nodded. Talking wasn't really what she wanted to do now, but she did have things she wanted to tell him.

Chapter 13

Penn hurried into his bedroom, undressing and tossing clothes as he went. The Kevlar battle gear was time-consuming to take off, but he did it in record time. He pulled a pair of jeans from his closet and a cobalt blue T-shirt from one of his drawers and rushed into the bathroom to wash his face and hands and redress.

Once he felt like himself again, he went back downstairs to find Livy in the living room. She'd been looking around, but there wasn't anything to see. The house was plain. Every wall was a cream color, with darker cream trim, and there were no photos on the walls. Penn hadn't lied when he'd said it came fully stocked. Sem had used a realtor to buy the place, hired a decorator to set it up with the bare bones of furniture, and then hired a shopping expert to stock the fridge, freezer, and pantry. The only thing Penn had done was bring his toys and clothes with him.

"Hey, sorry the place doesn't have more character, like yours," he said and walked over to take her bag from the sofa. "I'll just take this upstairs and be right back," he added and headed back up the stairs to place her bag on the cedar chest at the foot of his bed. He bounced back downstairs again and walked over to where she now sat on the sofa. He sat down beside her and took her hand in his.

"I know that I messed up by having Sem bespell

you. I'm sorry. It will never happen again," he said and brought her hand to his mouth for a kiss. "And please, just let me get this rest out? It feels like I've been waiting so long to tell you." He paused and smiled. When she nodded for him to go on and signaled that she'd keep her mouth closed by miming a zipper across her lips, he laughed. She had such a funny personality. It was just one of the things that he loved about her.

"I also wanted to tell you that I love you. I think I've loved you since the first time I saw you at your parents' funeral. I know that sounds wrong because it was a very sad time in your life, but I hope you understand it just *was it* for me. You filled a void in me, one I didn't know I had. I've fought this internal battle. I've argued with myself and tried talking myself out of being in love with you, but I can't do it. I also can't live with myself for putting you in danger."

"Why am I in danger?" Livy asked, and her brows drew together pensively.

"Because I love you, and I intend to make you mine," Penn explained. "And I refuse to let you go. Remember I told you what happened to all the Grigori mates and children? That's what I'm afraid of." He reached up and caressed her cheek. "I'd die if anything happened to you. I honestly don't know how any of my brethren carried on after they lost their loved ones."

He smiled and waited for what he said to sink in. After a few moments of silence, he grew worried. Livy just sat and stared at him. He'd just thrown a lot at her. Maybe she was just processing? His heart twisted in his chest at the thought of her plotting to run away from the crazy angel.

Finally, she smiled, and then she laid her head back

and started laughing, really laughing, with tears running from the corner of her eyes. Penn's heart sank, and he started to stand, but Livy refused to let go of his hand. She even pulled him back down to sit. She managed to stop laughing long enough to shake her head.

"I'm not laughing at you," she said and wiped her eyes. "I'm laughing because I've been so afraid to tell you the same thing. Well, not the same thing, but that I love you." She brought those big beautiful green eyes up to look him in the eye. "I adore you, too."

Penn stood and scooped her into his arms. He embraced her so tightly that she grunted a little.

"Sorry," he murmured and pulled back a smidgen. "I'm just so happy to hear you say that, but tell me, why were you afraid to tell me?" He took her hands and once again sat on the sofa, with her following suit.

"My reasons are a bit different. After losing Mom and Dad, I began to think that everyone I loved would eventually leave me, so why love you when you would just go back to your own life after all this was over? I was scared, Penn. You understand that feeling, don't you?"

Penn nodded, his eyes tearing from hurt at causing her any distress. He never wanted to see her scared or unhappy again. He also knew what it was like to live a misunderstood life.

"I understand. It looks like we both had some fears to work through," he murmured and pulled her into his lap. "At last, we're together now and never have to go through anything alone again. Will you stay with me?" he asked with his heart in his throat. If she said some bullshit about being independent, he was going to lose it.

But she surprised him by cupping his jaw and bringing his face to hers. She pressed her lips to his in a feather-light kiss and then moved to the other side of his jaw, where she pressed another kiss.

"Of course, I'll stay with you, but you must promise to stop being so over-protective. You can't do your job if you're constantly worrying about me and my safety. Can you do that?"

Penn furrowed his brows. "You mean you'd come back to the Compound with me? You'd come to Ireland to live with me and the rest of my family?" he asked and smiled. "Really?"

Livy laughed and wrapped her arms around his neck, pulling his lips to hers for another kiss.

"Yes. Besides an empty house, there's nothing for me here." Her head snapped up, and she frowned. "I can come to visit my parents' graves, right?"

"Of course. That's not even a question. Do you want to keep your house?" At this point, he'd promise her anything she wanted. He didn't know how they'd pull off closing the Nether doorway in her closet, and no other family could live in it like that, but they could figure that out later.

****

Livy smiled. Her heart was full of happiness. She had confessed her feelings, Penn had confessed his, and together they would build a life. She'd decided to go with him to his family's compound because, honestly, she wanted to go. She could finish her degree online. She could maybe even train with Barr and become a badass warrior herself. There was just so much to look forward to, and for once, in what felt like a long time, she was happy about her future. A future that Penn now offered her.

She looked back at him and smiled.

"We're doing this," she said. "We're really doing this." She pressed her lips to his in a light kiss that immediately took a turn for hot and steamy. Penn wrapped his arms around her waist and pulled her to straddle his hips. Every worry evaporated from her thoughts at the feel of his body against hers. He felt like Heaven and smelled like a pine forest after a rain.

His arms went around her, and she felt cherished, like the most important thing on earth. He pressed his lips to her neck, and chills spread across her body. She tilted her head back to give him better access. He moaned deep in his throat and lapped at the same skin he'd kissed with his tongue. The hot, slightly rough sensation had liquid heat pooling in her core. His mouth roamed around, his lips pressing feather-light kisses to spots here, there, and everywhere. Her pulse quickened.

Fire licked through her bloodstream, and she moved her hips, her body searching for a release from all the heat burning inside her.

Penn must have sensed her dilemma. He slipped her T-shirt over her head and smiled up at her before his hands went to her breasts. He kneaded them through the rough lace of her bra, the sensation sending little ripples of pleasure across them. He located her nipples and rolled them between his fingers, a slow, erotic rush that sent even more liquid heat coursing through her veins.

She closed her eyes, her breathing quickening. They'd had sex before, but this—this felt like making love to her. Every sensation that burst inside her was new, sexy, and forever branded in her mind and body.

"Shall we take this upstairs?" he asked, his voice seductive, a black magic spell, while his hands caressed every square inch of the satiny skin of her stomach, ribs, and chest. She couldn't think while his hands were everywhere, all at once. All she managed was a quick nod of her head.

She backed off him, giving him room to rise to his feet. He bent and literally swept her off her feet, and she let out a little squeak of surprise. She hoped that the rest of their lives was just like this, little surprises made of gestures one wouldn't think to expect. He strode to the stairwell, her body cradled softly in his arms.

Penn carried her straight to the bed, setting her on the edge of the massive California King. She lay back on the royal blue comforter and opened her arms for him. Instead of lying down with her, his deft fingers slid her socks off, then his hands went to her waist to remove her pants. As he peeled each leg down, he pressed kisses along the skin revealed.

Once her pants were off, he pulled his T-shirt off, and Livy's eyes widened at the flesh laid bare. Her mouth watered to lick every square inch of his glorious chest, then down over the six-pack abs, then even lower. He must have seen the love and lust shining in her eyes because he smiled and crawled up her body. His muscular frame pressed her into the mattress. His leg pushed hers apart. She gasped when she felt the evidence of his arousal pressed against her core.

His hands slid up over the curve of her breasts to frame her face.

"Do you have any idea how sexy you are?" he asked, his voice deep and husky.

She simply shook her head because she'd never

really thought about it. Then he lowered his head and pressed his lips to her forehead, her closed eyes, her nose, her jawline, then finally settled at the corner of her mouth.

"Kiss me, Livy. Kiss me like your life depended on it."

She did. She opened her mouth, her tongue slipping into his, and she reached up to cup his face. She slanted her head, and their tongues danced in a tornado of fury. They fed on each other's desire, exploring every square inch of each other's mouths, building heat until the flames almost consumed them both.

Suddenly, he tore his lips away and pressed kisses along her jaw, down her throat, to the valley between her breasts, then lingered over her heart a moment. His teeth grazed sensitive skin before they returned to her mouth.

"Lift your back," he said, his breath hot upon her lips, and she complied. His large hand slipped between her back and the bed, and within seconds, his long fingers had worked the hooks of her bra loose. He slowly slid the straps over her shoulders, his fingers leaving liquid fire in their wake. Her body ached and burned. Needed and hungered. With her naked chest pressed to his, she felt his heartbeat, so strong and comforting. Her own heartbeat struggled to time itself with his.

His skin was so hot, satisfyingly hot, and she moaned at the feel of his hard muscles against her womanly softness. It was like they were made for each other, their bodies fit together so perfectly.

He tossed her bra aside and lowered his lips to the

heated flesh of her chest. It was like she'd absorbed his warmth into herself. He took a breast in his hand, and his mouth lowered to the other. He kissed the flesh around her nipple while his hand immediately found the other and began kneading the bud between his fingers.

Livy climbed that mountain of pleasure. Everywhere his lips or hands touched sent a bolt of electricity coursing through her, and she couldn't do anything but ride the waves. Her body was his to command, his to love, his to bend to his own pleasure, but instead, he focused on giving her nirvana first. Desire pounded through her body and thundered in her ears.

His hand left her breast, going lower and lower still till it reached her cotton panties, his finger running beneath the hem, teasing the skin underneath. She writhed, her body unable to hold much more pressure before it exploded.

At last, he shimmied the underwear down over her hips and leaned back long enough to discard them on the floor along with his own jeans and underwear, and then they were laid bare against each other. He moved back up so that his lean, hard body hovered over her much smaller one. Their lips met again, and his hand found her most intimate part. He parted the moist curls and found the bud of flesh underneath. His finger massaged it, and Livy almost shot off the bed.

She swore she levitated, but instead of coming down, he pushed her even higher when his fingers traveled down to her core. One finger dipped in, then retracted, spreading the moistness until it covered her, and then he slid it back inside of her. She bore down on his finger, her body looking for that ever-elusive release, but he kept his hand just out of reach.

"Not so fast, my love," he murmured against her temple, his heated breath erotic against her earlobe. "I'm not done with you yet. I could love you for hours," he said and pressed a kiss to her ear, his tongue snaking out to grab her earlobe so that he could suckle it. She wouldn't make it hours; she'd barely held on this far.

Finally, after what seemed like hours of torment, Penn used his knee to push her thighs farther apart. He hovered over her and smiled down at her.

"Tell me you want me," he said, his voice husky. "Tell me you have to have me."

"I want you. I have to have you, like now," Livy said and smiled back at him, her hands going to his ass cheeks and pulling at him.

Penn chuckled, his smile turned triumphant, he slid into her, and their separate bodies became one. She moved her hands up to his hips and helped him as he glided in and out of her. Soon, she had the rhythm down and joined him in lifting her hips whenever he slid inside, causing him to go deeper and deeper.

The tension built and built. She laid her head back and closed her eyes, and little moans escaped her as he sped up, the friction all but sending her spiraling into oblivion. Before she could take any more, the orgasm was upon her, and she saw stars, her breath grew ragged, and her hands went to his face.

She leaned up and took his lips with her own, kissing him with all the pleasure he'd just given her. He moaned, and she felt him swell inside her, then he groaned, and he slowed down and eventually collapsed onto her, pressing their sweaty bodies together.

"I love you, Livy," he whispered into her ear.

She smiled and wrapped her arms around his neck. "I love you too, Penn," she said.

****

Penn wrapped his arms around Livy and rolled them until she sat atop him. They were still joined together, and he'd be lying if he said it wasn't erotic as hell. His heart galloped away in his chest, and his breath came in pants. He reached up and filled his palms with the two most glorious breasts he'd ever seen in his life. They were a handful, not too big and not too small, but perfect, just like the rest of her. And they were his for the rest of their lives.

He realized that the secret he'd been keeping from her wasn't his to keep anymore. He had to tell her before they went any further. He wouldn't have any secrets between them, not now and not ever.

"Livy, I need to tell you something," he said and continued to knead her breasts. "I won't have any secrets between us."

Livy leaned down and put her palms against his chest, holding herself upright. The saucy wench wiggled her hips, and he grew hard again. She was completely oblivious to the hold she had on his heart and now on his body.

"What is it?" she asked and trailed one finger over to his nipple. She grabbed it and rubbed it between her fingers, and tingles ran through his body. What was she doing to him? Whatever it was, he would gladly die like this. But, back to business.

"Here goes. Don't laugh," he warned. "You remember the first time we made love?"

"Hmm, how could I forget?"

"I was a virgin," he admitted, heat blossoming

across his cheeks.

Her eyes widened in surprise, but she didn't laugh. Instead, she smiled the most beautiful smile he'd ever seen. She leaned down to press her lips to his in a sweet, endearing kiss.

"You know I was as well," she said and moved to press a kiss to his cheek. "I never would have thought I'd been your first. You're so knowledgeable."

"Well." He blushed again. This confession was really going to be embarrassing. "I've had centuries to research and gain knowledge. I've read a lot of books in my life."

She didn't laugh at that either.

"So, you want to try some more hands-on?" she asked and wiggled her hips again. This time she rotated them and slid off, then back onto him, and he groaned.

"Boy, do I?" He laughed and pulled her down to lie against his chest. "Let's practice a little bit more before we go home."

The End…for now.

A word about the author…

L. D. Nash lives in the piney woods of Northern Louisiana with her husband, two grandsons, and entirely too many dogs. She's been writing in a broad range of genres for twenty-seven years. While dabbling in the world of indie publishing, she made Amazon's top ten bestseller list for "contemporary fantasy fiction." She spends all her free time either reading or writing. You can learn more about her at www.authorldnash.com

Thank you for purchasing
this publication of The Wild Rose Press, Inc.

For questions or more information
contact us at
info@thewildrosepress.com.

The Wild Rose Press, Inc.
www.thewildrosepress.com